THE PROMISE

Plan B

CORNELIA SMITH

THE VOW
Series

Copyright © 2016 by Cornelia Smith

Book Design by The Book Plug LLC

Presents

National Bestselling Author

Cornelia Smith

OTHER BOOKS BY CORNELIA SMITH

<u>www.thebookplug.com</u>

TABLE OF CONTENTS

CHAPTER 1

"Turn around. Lift up your hair," the deputy says.

Alisa has been booked for three hours. After moving from a holding cell to the second floor, she's being forced to undress and stand under a freezing-cold shower. Choking on tears, she meekly lifts her hair up while the female deputy sprays an awful-smelling liquid onto her body.

"Why couldn't this bitch just leave me alone?" Alisa manages to choke out. Being arrested is the most dehumanizing thing in the world, she thinks. She understands that she'd killed her husband, but didn't the fact that he cheated on her, broke her heart, and used her like a broom to sweep up the trash in his life, count for anything?

"We need to make sure that you don't expose any of the inmates to any new strains of head or pubic lice. We have enough problems controlling the strains that we have here already," the deputy says kindly. This woman doesn't look like she belongs in jail, the rookie thinks. But then again, neither did half of the male and female inmates. She Hands Alisa a pair of shower slippers and an orange jumpsuit large enough to accommodate two people, she waits while Alisa dresses slowly and blindly through her tears.

Vaguely, Alisa hears the two-way radio on the deputy's hip crackle. Watching as the woman walks away while talking into the radio, she takes a few minutes to try to compose herself. She feels like trash. Being treated like a common criminal. All for what, because a nosey DA couldn't let well enough be?

She will pay for this, if it's the last thing I do. On my dying bed, she will pay for this, Alisa thinks as tears slowly roll down her cheeks.

"People of the state of California versus Alisa Hopkins." The sheriff announces.

Hesitantly, Alisa rises from the hard bench.

"Back again?" Judge McCrary says.

"Unfortunately," Alisa murmurs back. Her spirit isn't as free as before and her facial expression isn't as blank as it was her first time in court. She now resembles a sad puppy as she stands before the judge with her lips poked out.

"Ms. Hopkins, you have been charged with section 187-199 the California penal code for attempted murder. Do you wave further reading of the complaint and complete statement of rights?"

Before James, Alisa's Jewish lawyer could whisper what to say to her, she uttered very softly,

"I do."

"And do you wish to enter a plea at this time?"

"Yes," Alisa answers.

"And how do you plea, Ms. Hopkins?" Judge McCrary asks.

"Not guilty Your Honor."

"You Honor, my client will like to request bail. Since her incarceration, she's been punished for information that shouldn't have been released by the police department," James Grier retorts.

"And what information is that?" Judge McCrary asks.

"My client informed Ms. Patterson that Monroe Gosling is Dawson's murderer and shortly after the information leaked my client has been threatened by inmates. The only person who is aware of this information besides Ms. Hopkins and me, is Ms. Patterson."

"You Honor, this is a complete setup. Ms. Hopkins knows that she is a high risk for bail, so this is her little plan to get a bail granted. No one is threatening her. I have not now, nor ever leaked information about my case to anyone. Just last night I was chased down by one of Ms. Hopkins' men; almost run off the road. She's playing games with the court and trying her best to intimidate me all at once," Patricia blurts.

"Did you call the police, Ms. Patterson?"

Patricia drops her head and murmurs, "No."

"You Honor, my client has been nothing but cooperative throughout this entire process. She wants her name cleared and for justice to be brought to the forefront like everyone else. Ms. Hopkins has no reason to run. She plans on fighting to the very end to clear her name. As far as Ms. Patterson's false accusation goes, Ms. Hopkins has no men, and she's been incarcerated which makes it almost impossible for her to torture Ms. Patterson in any form," James Grier argues.

Instantly, Patricia's blood boils. She sees where this is going and she's not too pleased. She can argue back and forth on how she's sure it was Alisa's men that ran her off the road, but she knows, it will only be considered hearsay in court without evidence.

"Bail denied," Judge McCrary replies before banging his gavel.

"Thank you, Your Honor," Patricia says surprised.

Happy, Patricia packs up her suitcase and heads for the door. Purposely, Alisa bumps into her on her way out. She whispers into her ear, "Let the games begin." Forcefully, Patricia shoves her away from her space with her shoulder.

"Move out of my way!" Patricia growls.

V
B

Alisa sits at a table with her head down. A single hanging light shines down on her. Patricia enters and sits in the chair directly across from her. She pulls a pack of cigarettes out and a lighter, then puts them on the table

"You need a smoke?" Patricia asks. Alisa shakes her head to deny the offer.

"To whom do I owe this pleasure?" Alisa jokes.

"Alisa, I know your husband hurt you. In fact, he cut you deep. I'm a woman, I know that pain all too well," Patricia stares deep into Alisa's glistening eyes as she speaks.

"I know you killed your husband and I understand why you did it. He played you like a video game. If you cooperate with me, I can make sure you don't do more than ten years in prison. You'll be on papers of course, but you'll be free." Patricia believes the deal she's offering is a slam dunk; Alisa would be crazy not to take it.

Alisa feels the complete opposite. Rudely, she bursts into laughter. She isn't taking any deal. She'll kill herself before she spends years in anybody's prison. "I didn't kill my husband. Monroe killed my husband." Stunned at Alisa's response, Patricia just shakes her head with disgust written all over her face.

"So, is that your plan? Are you kidding me right now?" Patricia replies.

"I don't have time for jokes kiddo, my life is on the line."

"And why on earth would she do that, huh? Why would she kill your husband, Ms. Hopkins?"

"Because, he wouldn't leave me for her," Alisa replies calmly without a smirk or smile on her face.

"I don't have time for this," Patricia gathers up her Manila folder and jumps up from the table.

"The deal is off, Ms. Hopkins. You had your chance," Patricia says on her way out.

CHAPTER 2

J ust as Patricia hangs her coat on the hall rack, a clown pops out from around the wall. He's as vivid as the gold confetti he blows out at her. Red hair as vibrant as fire on his head, starkly contrasting to the paper-white makeup of his face. His mouth is huge and raises into a smile. His steps have a bounce to them. Behind him, trails a mass of happy balloons, jostling in the brilliant rays, each as beautiful as the next. They read, *Congratulations Patricia*. Then Patricia spies his feet, clown feet. They are beyond large, at least twice the length of an ordinary shoe, slapping onto the hardwood floor like flippers.

Jason sees the shock register on Patricia's face before she can hide it. A small smile plays on his lips; he's confident the surprise will win Patricia over.

"I know you always wanted a clown for your birthday, and I know it's not your birthday, but you did win The Grim Reaper trial, one of the biggest murder cases of the decade and you just put Alisa behind bars. So, I thought what the heck! I'll get her a clown just because."

Tears would drip from Patricia's eyes if she blinked. She's overwhelmed. It isn't what Jason said though; his words are like vanilla pudding, sweet in their ordinary sort of way, it's the richness of his tones – luxurious and the warm thought of him thinking of her. Patricia's face washes blank with confusion, it's like her brain cogs couldn't turn fast enough to take in the information from her wide eyes. Every muscle of her body freezes before a grin creeps onto her face. It soon stretches from one side to the other, showing every single tooth.

"Congratulations!"

Every friend, neighbor, and co-worker creeps in quietly from the kitchen. Apparently, Patricia is hot-shit and she didn't get the memo. Who'd have thought she'd have *The Hawk* himself, Koch, and Jason in one room? She'd given Jason his spare key back but not once did she think to get hers back in return. At that very moment, she's happy she didn't. She deserves to get her ass kissed for a while and Jason having her key surprisingly, is a blessing in disguise.

"Oh, my goodness, where did you find these strangers?" Patricia jokes. As she makes her way through the house hugging new and old faces. Everyone congratulates her on her big win, and of course *The Hawk* personally offers Patricia her job back. The celebration goes on into the night, everyone is dancing like they'd forgotten how to stand still. Jason is moving like his limbs are made of spaghetti and Patricia's face is an epic picture of pure excitement. They're enjoying the night and little did Patricia know the night is only going to get better.

She throws her hands up and makes her way to the floor when her favorite song by Bruno Mars comes on.

"Hey, that's my song right there!" she yells out as she moves her curves from one side to another.

It's a beautiful night,

We're looking for something dumb to do.

Hey baby,

I think I wanna marry you.

Patricia sings along with Bruno. She's so occupied with calculating her moves, it takes a minute for her to notice the party-goers meticulously choreographed routine on the dance floor. They are making hearts with their hands and singing to Patricia for Jason. The entire party sings along with the soundtrack by Bruno Mars as Jason makes his way down to the floor on one knee.

Loudly, the party continues to sing to Patricia, *"It's a beautiful night. We're looking for something dumb to do. Hey baby, I think I wanna marry you."*

Tears drip from Patricia's eyes. She covers her mouth with both her hands. She's stunned, a proposal is the last thing she expected from Jason.

Choking on his tears, Jason confidently says, "I love you, Patricia, and I know you're the one for me. It will mean the world to me if you'll join me in this thing called life. Patricia, will you be my wife, will you marry me?"

The party that was once loud and in an uproar is now silent as a mouse. Patiently, they wait on an answer from Patricia. Her lips are shivering, her hands are shaking, and her tears are running.

Finally, after twenty-long seconds Patricia replies, "Yes, I'll marry you man."

The party cheers in unison as Jason places the fourteen-carat ring onto Patricia's finger. Tightly, the two hug each other. They kiss for what seems to be an eternity.

"So, shall it stay put?" Patricia asks with a smile eternally stained upon her lips.

"Shall what stay put?" Jason replies.

"This joy, this love, this laughter, this feeling."

"Yes, little lady. I will spend the rest of my days catering to our love." The celebration is a riot of color, everyone a little more hyped up than before. Patricia's eyes eat up the scene, she's overwhelmed and a little tipsy. Her limbs are supercharged, and her hips are rocking. Everything about Bruno Mars makes her want to dance; her feet moving with grace and her heart beating with joy. For hours, this goes on and then finally, people begin to fade. One by one, the party grows thin until there is no one left standing but the two love birds.

"I can't wait to rip you out of that suit," Jason murmurs into Patricia's ear. They're still pressed tightly together as one in one another's arms, swaying from side-to-side.

"Are you sure you're ready for this?" Patricia asks.

"Baby, I was born ready," Jason replies without second thought.

"No, I'm not talking about that, you horny man," Patricia bursts into laughter.

"I'm talking about marriage: life with me, the picket white fence, the whole nine."

"Like I said, I was born ready," Jason brags. He takes her face in his hands and lifts it until she is lost in his eyes. He starts with her forehead. Short, sweet, tender kisses. His lips move down to the ridge of her nose and glide down slowly and methodically until they find hers. Patricia's mouth gratefully and hungrily accepts Jason's tongue without hesitation. Before she knows it, she is totally engrossed in his arms and he in hers.

Their kisses become deeper. The next thing Patricia knows, Jason has her up against the wall with her legs straddled around his waist, and her blazer is toppling to the floor. Then the kisses stop as suddenly as they begin.

He puts her back down on the floor gently and takes her hand.

"Follow me," he whispers.

"I will follow you anywhere."

He led her upstairs into the master bathroom and then shut the door. Patricia assumes he wants to take a shower or bath together. Much to her surprise, he twirls her around until they are both facing the full-length mirror on the back of the door.

"Why don't you like sex with the light on, Patricia?" He reaches around her and starts unbuttoning her blouse. "You're so incredibly beautiful."

Patricia stands there, frozen, and glares in the mirror while he seductively removes all of her clothing, nibbling on her neck and shoulder blades while he goes about his task. Once she is entirely nude, he takes her large breasts into his palms and rubs her hard nipples between his thumbs and forefingers.

One of his hands drops down and finds the cherry between her thighs. She's in a trance, somewhere between reality and heaven's gate. His fingers work magic on her clit and explore her pussy lips with a tenderness she's never felt.

"You will be mine for a lifetime, and during that lifetime, I want to see all of you. The real you. Walk with me out your comfort zone. Let me take some pictures of this beautiful artwork."

Patricia is super nervous, but at this very moment, she's so much into Jason that even taking pictures is acceptable. Posing in the nude is something she's never imagined doing. Hell, she has never even wanted to pose with clothes on. For Jason, she's not only willing, but eager to please him.

"Okay," she replies, taking hold of the hand between her legs and guiding his fingers deeper into her. She stares at him in the mirror.

"Take my picture." They leave the bathroom, and he lays her down on the bed. It's covered with cotton sheets. He removes the pins from her hair, letting it flow down around her shoulders. He bends over and kisses her.

"Wait right here, baby." He leaves to get his iPhone out his coat pocket, and while he is gone, she plays with her nipples. She's never masturbated in front of a man before, but she didn't stop when he reentered the room. In fact, she puts on a show for him.

She masturbates while he takes pictures of her. She's shocked at her actions and feels sort of slutty but that doesn't stop her. She doesn't look at the camera. She shut her eyes and pretends it's his hands on her breasts and fingering her pussy. She imagines him taking her right there in her room, on her bed, grabbing her full hips and pulling them deeper onto his dick, partaking of her from the front and then the back. Patricia imagines him suckling on her nipples and nibbling on her ass cheeks. She imagines him sliding his thick dick in and out of her mouth, and his cum trickling out of the sides and down her chin, splattering on her breasts.

As she imagines it all, she cums all over the cotton sheets. She comes like she has never before. He snaps one last picture, and then she hears the humming. She opens her eyes, she's shocked to see that he is naked. She doesn't remember hearing him undress. She licks her lips seductively, as she partakes of the beautiful view. Jason's body is beautiful, more like perfect, and Patricia is flattered that he now belongs to her. She sits up on the bed and reaches out her arms for him. He puts the phone down on the foot of the bed and joins her. The two makes sweet love all night long. They do all the things Patricia dreamed of during her lonely nights.

CHAPTER 3

The buzzer of the extension phone goes off like an annoying rattlesnake. Monica scoops it up, says, "Hello," listens for a moment, and then replies, "Are you sure, Alisa?"

"Just do it!" Alisa snaps back before ending the call. As soon as she turns from the payphone, she's greeted by her angry roommate.

"I told you not to try me, bitch! You been in my shit, haven't you?" Snake-like veins swivel across Robin's forehead as she shrieks out her frustration.

"No, I don't want to try you," Alisa murmurs.

"Bitch, you think you can put a murder on a police officer and get away with the shit? You must think the world revolves around you!" Silently, Alisa shakes her head, while keeping her eyes on Robin's hand movements.

"You come all up in here, steal my shit, and think you can just get away with it?" Robin continues to yell out. Before Alisa can utter another word, Robin throws four blows.

A sudden gush of pain jolts throughout Alisa's body. Her stomach aches, her arms lose tension, and her legs begin to weaken.

She will not get the better of me, Alisa thinks as she drops to the ground. Her tongue soaks in the taste of blood.

Bruised and breathless, with a leg in agony, Alisa doesn't bother getting up. Robin grabs Alisa by the foot and pulls her toward their room. Alisa's head is pounding. Robin brings a fist to her face once more, snapping her nose into a grotesque shape.

"That'll teach her ass Robin!"

The inmate's voice is the last thing Alisa hears before blanking out.

When the dawn comes, Alisa can barely move, and not because she had a good night's sleep. Every muscle has seized up. Her body is struggling to recover; to repair the damages. Unable to move with any grace, her movements are jerky. Robin wakes sleepily when she feels Alisa rise from her bunk.

"Are you okay?" she mumbles.

"I said kick my ass, not kill me." Alisa edges into the light that flows like water through the small window and strips off her topmost layer. On each arm, there are great purple welts that will only deepen over the coming week. Against her chocolatey skin, they are ridiculous, but she's satisfied with Robin's work.

"You better be glad you didn't break any of my bones," Alisa admonishes Robin.

"I had to make it look real, isn't that what you wanted?" Robin is trying not to stare at Alisa's nose, but she keeps finding her eyes diverting to it. One minute they are obediently on her red-rimmed eyes and the next they are resting on the bloody mess that had been a perfectly ordinary nose only hours before she destroyed it. So ordinary, she could not recall what it had looked like before the beating.

"Look at my face! Shit!" Alisa grumbles.

"You don't look all that bad," Robin responds.

"Who you think you talking to? A dummy? You know my face is as purple as my damn arms!" Alisa barks. "But, it's perfect. You did a good job."

Sluggishly, Robin places her back to the wall. "So why did you need me to beat you? I don't get it," Robin asks.

"Don't ask questions you don't want answers to," Alisa replies as she wobbles back to her bunk.

"I thought for sure, I wouldn't see you back in here again," Robin says.

"Well, you can bet your life, this is the last time." Alisa sips on the bottle of water she bought from commissary.

"The beating must be a part of plan B."

Robin hits a nerve and Alisa snaps, "What plan?"

"You must have a second plan, since your first one didn't work out." Initially, Alisa wants to snap but then she remembers how easy it is to distract Robin. Quickly, she turns the table.

"So why are you still here? I thought Mr. Hot Shot lawyer was going to get you out?"

"He's working on it," Robin replies.

"What are you in for anyway?" Alisa asks. For a moment, Robin gets lost in a daze. She thinks about the very incident that landed her a bed in the house of hell.

"Love. I trusted a man with my heart, my child's safety, and my life. He robbed a store and didn't tell me. I was out in the car with my baby, waiting on him to come out with some snacks and an Arizona Iced Tea, but this nigga came out with the whole register instead."

"So, what does that have to do with you? You didn't rob the store," Alisa says.

"Yeah, but I didn't tell them he did it, either. So, they locked us both up and took my baby to DFCS." Warm tears slowly roll down Robin's cheeks as she recalls the sweet sound of her baby girl's laugh. Her innocent giggles haunt her memory.

Mission accomplished, Alisa thinks as she looks over at Robin's stunned face. Alisa lays flat on her back, resting the back of her head on her hands.

"You'll be fine, but I hope for your daughter's sake. You've learned your lesson."

Swiftly, Robin wipes her tears and says, "Oh, I have. You don't have to worry about that."

"I might have a way you can make some money. You know, a little something to get you on your feet when we're released from this hell hole."

A smile creeps up on Robin's face. She turns to Alisa and says, "Are you serious? Don't play with me, Alisa."

Amused, Alisa giggles. "Sweetie, my word is all I have as a woman."

CHAPTER 4

Flora and animal prints compete with loud plaids and stripes for Patricia's undivided attention. Throwing her arms up in disgust, she stomps over to a full-length mirror placed on a dressing room door.

She stares at the mirror, and a large, but very attractive, young lady stares back. She's warm, with light brown eyes, a bomb ass weave, and a killer smile. Patricia admires this woman. She feels like herself again, she feels like she's the best damn thing walking around LA.

"Damn, I look good, but not in this ugly ass outfit!" Patricia blurts out.

"Whatcha looking for?"

Jumping at the voice that shocks her out of her thoughts, Patricia turns around to Jamellah grinning at her.

"I've been up and down this store three times and I didn't see your big ass!" Jamellah jokes.

"I was hiding over there, in the prints. I swear, these buyers must want us big women to look like big, beautiful tents. Look at this shit!" Patricia exclaims, motioning to the clothes around her. Flipping through a rack of clothes, Jamellah's face soon adopts a mask of heavy disgust. The prints and colors do nothing for any figure; not even a stick figure.

"Ewwweee! Why are we even looking in this store? There has to be at least a million other places in LA to shop besides this one. Unless your goal is to look like Monique off the *Parkers*." The girls burst into laughter.

"Oh, now you know you're wrong for that one," Patricia replies.

"I suggest, you find somewhere else to shop because this my friend isn't the move." Jamellah flips through a couple more of the pieces before finally calling it quits.

"I guess we can go. I usually find some cute things in here. Maybe they changed buyers or something. Then again, I might have gained weight since the last time I shopped in here, which is forcing me to look at this hideous section." Slinging her purse over her shoulder, Patricia led the way out of Plus Size Paradise.

"Wait! Look at this dress!" Jamellah exclaims.

"Better yet, look at the price!"

"Dang…. How much is it? Patricia asks, examining the nicely cut linen dress.

"Thirty percent off the ticket price. Here, go try it on." Jamellah hands over the dress to Patricia.

Walking toward the dressing room, Patricia holds the red dress close as if it's her new best friend. Closing the door and removing her jumper, she slides the dress over her suitable physique. It slides down her curves and rest several inches above her knees. The crisply fancy silk does wonders for her large bust line, while the ruffle peplum waist takes inches off her thick midsection. Twirling around, she feels and looks like the confident woman she knows all too well. She knows Jason is going to have a fit when he sees how short the dress is, but he'll still enjoy every second of it. She's found the newest addition to her feel-good look good wardrobe.

The door to the dressing room swings open and out walks a new-found woman, in Jamellah's opinion.

"Love looks good on you girl. I'm so happy for you."

Patricia flashes her pearly white teeth. "Thank you, girl, I'm really excited about this new phase." Love has boosted Patricia's confidence, she feels sexier, more confident and heart healthy. Spinning round once again, she gives Jamellah a good view of the great dress and all it does for her figure. Overcome with emotion, Jamellah runs up to her friend and gives her a big, tight, suffocating hug.

"I'm so happy for you. You deserve all the joys of the world," Jamellah replies. The salesgirl looks on in a state of confusion while Patricia and Jamellah hold onto each other while allowing the happy tears to flow. Looking at each other's faces, the girls know that no words nor explanations are needed for the show of emotion.

"Now that I got you in a good mood, can you get this bag for me?" Jamellah jokes.

"Yes, cow." Linking her arms with Patricia's, the two skip toward the cash register area to pay for their items like they're teenage girls.

The salesgirl, who's clearly on break, flips through channels looking for her VH1 Love and Hip-Hop.

"I thought you said they play the reruns today, Layla?" The young girl's eyes are pasted to the flat screen mounted on the wall behind the cash register.

She flips past CNN, MSNBC, and FOX 5.

"Hold up, go back." Patricia is appalled when she glances up at the television to see a beautiful picture of Alisa pop-up.

"What the fuck!" she yells as she grabs the remote from the salesgirl and turns up the volume. She listens as the plastic-face blonde yaps away about Monroe being Dawson's alleged killer. She then goes on about Alisa being a victim to police harassment and how she's being tortured in jail because of Monroe's premature death. The pictures of Alisa's face are horrific. Any decent person would find them discouraging and sympathize with her.

"Here's your change!" the salesgirl says to Patricia.

"Is this bad?" Jamellah asks.

"It's worse than bad!" Patricia snaps strutting out the store.

"Damn, this bitch never stops, does she?" Jamellah barks following behind Patricia closely. "Don't let it stress you, Pat. You got this. There's no way she's getting out of this one."

In the back of Patricia's mind, she's thinking, *it's never that simple with this bitch.*

"Listen, you got your job back; you're about to be married soon. You got a lot of good shit going for you. Don't let this crazy bitch steal your joy," Jamellah says as they load their bags in Patricia's truck.

"Yeah, you right. I'm not about to let this bitch steal my joy. I got an engagement dinner to plan."

"Aww! Bitch you getting married!" Jamellah screams at Pat as she puts the car in drive.

"Iss getting married!" Pat yells out her window.

CHAPTER 5

The gang steps forward with confidence. They don't want Robin; they want Alisa and their history proves that they aren't friends. They expect easy pickings; that Robin will give Alisa up without a fight. Alisa's brain is racing for ways out.

There are four of them. I can cut one or two of them and maybe the others will back off, Alisa thinks.

Robin sees that Alisa is traumatized, and in her opinion, she's not the person everyone thinks she is. She's a gentle flower; loving, caring, and she's just been through a lot in her life. Since alive is better than dead, Robin tells her to follow her lead. At that moment, Robin realizes how foolish it was to stage that fight. The stunt made Alisa new bait.

I can cut up three of them and hopefully, Ms. Crazy can handle the other, Robin thinks. The odds are on their side, but Robin likes surety when it comes to her life. She has a daughter to get home to.

"I'm not going to die in jail," Robin mumbles to Alisa. She tenses her legs and draws out her blade. Alisa does the same. Robin said a prayer silently, *Please Lord cover me with your blood and keep me safe.* Then from nowhere, another gang circles them. The cafeteria is starting to look like a war zone.

"Yo, Alisa! What you got for me?" the big red dyke yells.

"It's not even that type of party, Big Red," Robin says.

"Oh, this bitch is going to have to pay up, Robin. Dawson was my nigga. We worked out together, shot ball together. It's no way I'm just going to let his motha-fuckin' killer just parlay up in this bitch without consequences."

Alisa giggles. *She's a joke*, she thinks. It didn't matter how out-numbered she and Robin are, biting her tongue or bowing down just isn't an option.

"Oh, something funny bitch?" Big Red charges towards Alisa and before she can make it too close, she's stopped by Robin's hand.

"I told you it's not that type of party, Big Red. Chill."

Robin is no beast, if size is the judge. She's pretty in the face; thin in the waist with thick thighs. She stands at five foot seven and she's not half as muscular as Big Red, but, she hails straight out of Chesterfield Square. Her hood makes Compton look like the suburbs. Survival is a must there, and everywhere she goes, she carries that trait.

"Don't tell me you were fucking my husband too?" Alisa blurts out with an annoying smirk on her face.

"That bitch thinks this shit is a game, cuz," one member of Big Red's posse utters, rubbing her chin as if there was a beard growing beneath it.

"Fuck it! If Robin wants to play bodyguard, we'll get that bitch too!" another member from the posse, who's sporting a million and two tattoos, yells.

In that frozen second between stand off and fighting, Robin sees the gang's eyes flick from her to Alisa. She and Alisa's faces are unreadable; no fear, no invitational smirk. Robin is banking on them making the mistake she predicts they would minutes ago, and they do. In that instant, they charge at her, ignoring Alisa, thinking Robin is protecting her *meal ticket*.

They expect it to be five on one, over in a bloody flash, and then they go back to their cell. The plan is not to kill her, but to teach her and Alisa a lesson with one beating. But things don't go their way, not at all. In seconds, Robin has taken two and Alisa three. The tile floor stains darkly with their blood. No butcher in sight, just expertly sliced jugulars.

Robin looks at Alisa, still emotionless and very impressed. Her skills are flawless, despite this being her first jail fight. There is no pleasure in her face, as Robin never expects there to be, and tonight there will be victory to celebrate.

Alisa and Robin chop it up about almost everything; men, clothes, and old friends. Robin is devouring the many snacks Alisa has awarded her with. Their talk is littered with smiles. There is real communication amongst the two, not just words but Alisa is very careful about the stories she shares. She's doing more listening than talking. Their chemistry is an ignored sign of growing love. It's as obvious as the morning sun, as real as the grass. The feeling flows through them as their conversation fills the air. The two talk until they are out of stories and energy.

CHAPTER 6

"**S**low down, Chelsey! You're speeding!"

Achton and Chelsey are speeding down San Bernardino Freeway I-10; they're on their way to the jail. Achton has been a nervous wreck since Chelsey got behind the wheel thirty-eight minutes ago. If it wasn't for the vast backdrop of buildings, Adele CD, and the outlet malls, he probably wouldn't be able to stand the roller-coaster of a ride.

"I'm not speeding, Dad! I'm only doing sixty-five. And what's that you're reading? Not those dreadful poems you got from those desperate housewives; I hope."

Achton drops the piece paper in his lap. "You mean to tell me you've been reading my letters?" Achton questions.

"No. But you left them on the dinner table one day, and I couldn't help but read some of them. I cracked up."

"What is so funny?"

"They are corny, daddy. They sound so desperate. '*Achton, if you need anything—a foot rub, a friend, or a meal, call me*,'" Chelsey mimics. "Get real. Don't tell me you're falling for the game, Dad."

"I thought they were very thoughtful," Achton says.

"Okay, daddy. If you think so. But why are we going to the jail, again?"

Hesitantly, Achton murmurs, "I'm going to visit Alisa."

"What?" Chelsey turns to face Achton.

"Keep your eyes on the road, Chelsey. You're not that good of a driver, baby girl."

"I got the wheel, daddy. Don't worry about that. Do you want to fill me in a little on this visitation?"

"Not really. I'll give you a little info, but that's all."

"That's not fair, dad. You aren't the only one who lost mom. I deserve to be filled in; to know what you know," Chelsey whines.

"Do you want to take a little information for five hundred or no information for a thousand?" Achton jokes.

"Okay, spill," Chelsey says.

"Alisa's been writing me, asking that I come and see her. She's not telling me what she wants but she assures me, it's something I want to hear. I feel like I owe it to your mother to see what it is that she wants."

Heavily, Chelsey sighs. "Is that it?" she questions.

"Yes, that's it; for now," he replies. Achton suddenly feels like he's walked into an oven set at five hundred degrees, so he reaches to turn the air up as high as it will go. He fans himself with the desperate housewives' letters. Beads of sweat magically forms across his forehead. More starts dripping over his eyelids and temples. He absolutely hates when he gets nervous.

They're getting closer to the jail and his nerves are all over the place. He can't control them. Achton doesn't know what to expect from Alisa. He's heard so many things about her from the news and Monroe. He secretly prays he's able to control his anger when he sees her because it will be a sad case for Chelsey to lose both of her parents.

"So, are you nervous, dad?" Achton looks to the left of him and for ten long seconds, he stares Chelsey down with a funny look in his eyes.

"I don't get scared sweetheart," he lies.

"What are you going to ask her? Do you even know?"

"No, I don't have a blueprint. I'm just going to Jay-z this thing, get it?" Both Chelsey and Achton burst into laughter at his corny joke.

"I wonder what she's like," Chelsey murmurs.

"Well, I don't know what she is like, but I do know she is human just like you and me," Achton says.

"Well, that certainly narrows things down. Dad, turn the air down a little, please. It's freezing in here."

"I'm sorry, baby girl," Achton reaches over to turn the air down some, even though the air was just beginning to kick in good enough to cool him down.

"Did you save me some chilly?" Chelsey changes the subject and asks.

"Of course, I did. You're going to love it too. The desperate housewives out did themselves." Chelsey giggles.

"Well you're here, Ms. Daisy," Chelsey jokes.

"Chelsey, don't go far, don't speed, and don't go far."

"Dad, chill. You're saying the same thing twice. I'm not going too far. I'm going to go grab something to eat and wait for your call."

Achton stares Chelsey down for twenty seconds and then hesitantly shuts the car door. Before walking off, he sticks his head into the window and says again, "Don't go far Chelsey and don't speed."

"Okay, dad. Now go before you miss visitation or something like that."

When Achton lifts his head at last to face Alisa, there is no trace of tears in his eyes, nor any track marks on his reddening face. His eyes are narrow, rigid, cold, and hard.

In that moment, Alisa knows Achton is far away and she must pull him in. It's clear she's the enemy. The trend of moving from the most loved to the most hated would be the end of a weaker woman, but Alisa is far from *weak*.

Achton's energy is all bad, Alisa didn't feel even one good vibration. She draws in a deep breath as she reminds herself that the burning hard stare will last only as long as it takes her to think of the most brutal, cutting thing she can to assassinate her character. After that, they can get over the obvious and onto forgiving and building, *perhaps*. It's so hard to tell and yet pointless not to try.

"I'm a bitch, when it comes to my work."

Achton is confused on Alisa's direction for this conversation. He stares at her with a puzzled face, wondering, *what does this have to do with me?*

"I'm an introvert, so I don't have many friends. I don't love easy, but I love hard. I'm a selfish type of girl when it comes to the things I love, but yet and still, I will give my last." Still confused on Alisa's direction, Achton finds the facts Alisa is stating about herself also define him.

"Long story short, I'm a lot of things but a killer isn't one." On cue, tears flow from Alisa's beautiful brown eyes.

"I know you're probably wondering why I'm telling you all of this." Silently, with no remorse Achton nods his head *yes*.

"I'm telling you all this because whether you believe me or not, I think it's only right you hear the truth from me before things blow-up in the media. For the longest, they have kept you in the dark about this whole ordeal, by them I mean the police department. Including your wife, Monroe. They've managed to keep the truth from the media but all of that is about to change." Attentively, Achton is listening.

"We tend to love people for who we know them to be and not for who they really are." Slowly, Alisa slides a manila folder over to Achton.

"They were in love with each other. They were planning on leaving us for one another."

Curiously, Achton opens the folder to the jaw-dropping pictures. There in his hands, he holds pictures of his naked wife and a built black man, making what seems to be sweet love. They're so explicit, he wants to vomit.

"They were planning on leaving us until I got in their way. You see my unfaithful husband forgot one little thing before he made those promises to his mistress: if he left me, he also left everything that comes with me. The money, cars, clothes, businesses; the whole nine. Once he figured there was no way he could leave me and take the money with him, he decided leaving his wife wasn't the best option for him."

Achton's wet blue eyes light with fire.

"When Dawson dropped little Ms. Monroe, she reached out to me, hoping I would leave my husband. I told her; I wouldn't dare."

Everything is starting to make sense to Achton. He's turned a blind eye to a lot when it came to Monroe's wrongdoing, but he's no dummy. Nothing Monroe told him is adding up now. She promised him it was Dawson who wouldn't let her be because he was so in love with her. From the looks of things, Achton is starting to believe it's the other way around. *The suicide makes sense now.*

"She was so angry that he wouldn't leave me, she threatened me. She used her badge…"

Before Alisa can complete her sentence. Achton jumps up from the table, grabs the pictures and jets for the door. Before he leaves he mumbles out, "I don't want to hear another word of this."

"Well, when you are ready for the whole truth, you know where to find me."

Alisa feels good about the meeting. She knows Dawson will be back. He'll be chasing sleep until he gets answers.

"You know that job I was telling you about?"

Robin rolls over on her side to face Alisa, "Yeah, what about it? It is a green light?"

"It's definitely a green light, and if you do it right, you won't have to worry about money. I'll make sure you and your daughter are good. But if you fuck up..."

"You don't have to tell me what will happen, Alisa. I think I know you by now. I got you. No holes, no leaks, no fuck-ups! You looking out for me, so you know I'm not going to fuck this up for you." Robin turns back over on her left side facing the wall. "Ole girl, gotta lot of enemies," she mumbles.

"What you say?" Alisa asks.

"Oh nothing," Robin responds.

"Goodnight."

"Yeah, yeah. Go to sleep."

Alisa isn't the type for mushy affection, but Robin continues to give it to her anyway.

CHAPTER 7

The party that Patricia assumes she's late for is still in full affect. The celebration seems to be aiming for an all-nighter. Everyone is dancing like they'd forgotten how to stand still. Jason is moving like his limbs are made of spaghetti. There is a group of blood-sucking ticks surrounding him. At least, that's how Patricia views the thin blondes dancing with Jason juggling their fake boobs in his face and flaunting their Barbie like curves in their skin-tight dresses.

Patricia face is an epic picture of pure disappointment. She wants to walk over to Jason and beat the shit out of him but everyone who works at *The Hawk* is here. Jason helped win a big case and the firm is celebrating. Things only going to get better from here on out for Jason's career with *The Hawk,* but if he didn't get it together, his relationship isn't going to be as successful.

Patricia struts over to Jason on the dance floor. Her knuckles her red from clenching her fist too hard. She grits her teeth in effort to remain silent. Her frustration builds anger within and it's like acid – burning at her insides. Her face is red with suppressed rage when she locks eyes with Jason. He knows she is pissed. It looks like Patricia is gearing up to hit one of the girls. Quickly, Jason stops Patricia in her tracks with one hand pressed against her shoulder. She swings his hand away and then confronts him in front of his groupies.

"Really, Jason?" she barks.

"Chill, woman. I'm just dancing," he tries to joke away the situation, but Patricia isn't laughing.

"You just have no shame, Jason. None whatsoever." The blood-sucking ticks are still in motion. It's like Patricia isn't even standing before them. They're even dancing around her.

"Excuse me ladies," Jason says, as he pulls Patricia off the dance floor and out into the hall.

"You just insist on embarrassing me, don't you?" Jason says, with his hand wrapped around Patricia's arm.

"Embarrassing you?" she barks.

"Yes, this is our workplace," Jason snaps.

"Exactly, Jason. This is our workplace; you should act like you know that. You up in here dancing all around these groupie bitches and shit."

Jason places his index finger over his lips and says, "Shhh!"

"Watch your damn mouth. I hate you speaking that way. You're acting like a classless hood rat."

Patricia bites her tongue while some of the senior partners pass through the hall. As soon as they are out of sight she yells, "Fuck you, Jason!" Quickly, she runs to catch the elevator.

Patricia struts off the elevator and into the parking garage. There is no one in sight yet Patricia feels like she's being watched.

"Shit, where did I park?" she mumbles as she blindly scuffles through her purse for her keys. The sounds are getting closer. Patricia makes a three-sixty turn in the middle of the parking deck; still she sees not a soul. How many times has she seen this scene in a movie? *Too many,* she thinks before increasing her speed.

"Fuck, where are those fucking keys?"

She continues to search in her purse for her car keys and then out the blue, a man dressed in all black appears. He stands stiff; staring blankly from the aisle over from Patricia. His silence freaks her out, so she decides to run down the aisle she assumes she parked down. Her feet slip outwards on the wet parking deck floor as she turns the corner, the cold evening air is shocking her throat and lungs as she inhales deeper, faster. With each footfall, a jarring pain shoots from her ankle to knee.

Patricia's heels are no good to her right now. As she kicks them off, her heart beats faster and the adrenaline demands she run, right now, no delay, but unless she gets them off, she can't. She wishes to God they were workable but they're three inches high. Then the cold, wet floor makes matters worse. Her feet slip and she almost tumbles over; something she cannot afford. Patricia hears the tall, mysterious man dangling keys getting closer, and she is no longer confused about his actions. He's definitely chasing her. He's now running down the same narrow path. She prays for someone to walk off the elevator. Before Patricia knows it, she decides to scream. Her voice rips through the air; the desperation in it scares her.

"Help me!"

She sounds like someone in a movie. She keeps running towards her truck. She now has her sight on the Rover, she must make it to the SUV before Mr. Man makes it to her. As soon as she gets the car door open she feels a hand grasp at her dress. Quickly, she jumps in the truck, slams the door, and locks it. *This is all Alisa's doing*, she assumes before scurrying out the parking garage. As Patricia speeds down the deserted streets in attempt to lose Mr. Man, it hit her; it could be anyone chasing her. She'd helped put away so many bad guys; it would be almost impossible for her to guess who's out to get her.

At her front door, Patricia wipes a hand across her cheek, smooths the last tear away, then slides the key into the lock. When she turns it, the tumbler inside doesn't move. She twists the knob and it opens. The door is not locked.

She quickly recounts her movements before leaving and is positive she locked the door. That can mean only two things: someone has broken in or Jason has beat her home. Patricia quietly pushes through the door, hurries into the living room, and stops. She stands silent, feeling a presence in the house.

"Jason? Is that you?" Patricia calls out, she can feel her heart pounding in her chest.

"Up here!" she hears him call, his voice muffled by distance and walls.

Patricia takes the stairs quickly, pulling herself up two at a time. Across from the bedroom is Patricia's home office. The door is slightly ajar. Patricia stops just in front of it to take a deep breath, she tries to suppress the fear on her face, telling herself everything is okay. She pushes the door open and before she can say anything, tears leak from her beautiful brown eyes and she begins to sob.

"What is wrong with you now, woman?" Jason jumps up from the desk chair and walks over to Patricia. "Are you telling me, you're going to start a fight and then play victim?"

Jason wraps his hands around Patricia. He assumes she's just being an emotional baby. *Maybe she's on her period,* he thinks. Her whimpering increases and now, he's curious. "What, Patricia? What?" he barks.

"Why didn't you answer your phone? I called on my way here," she whimpers out.

"Because I was mad with you. We did just get into an argument, you know."

Patricia cries harder.

"Okay, okay. I'm not mad with you anymore," Jason says.

"It's not that," she muffles out between sniffles.

"Then what is it, Patricia? I don't feel like playing *guess Patricia's problem* today."

"I was chased down by some man. I think Alisa sent him."

"What?" Jason yells, pulling back from Patricia. "Who chased you?" Green snake-like veins are vividly popping out the side of his neck.

"Some man. He was waiting for me when I got off the elevator at work. He chased me. He started following me, but I think I lost him."

Jason is furious, and he now feels guilty for not answering the phone for Patricia when she called. He called himself making her pay for her behavior, but it turns out he's the only one paying for his selfish ways. This is the day he'd wished he parked in the parking deck instead of the streets. At least then he could've caught the guy because he left out the building right after Patricia did.

"Come on, Pat. Let me get you in the bed." He leads Patricia to the room, undresses her, and then tucks her in bed.

"Where are you going?" She turns to her side to face Jason who's standing in the door.

"I need to go handle some things. I got to get a handle on this shit."

"Jason!"

"Get some rest, Patricia. I'll be back." Jason dashes out the room, down the stairs, and out the door.

CHAPTER 8

Alisa treads in the court room a bloody mess. Her face is grotesque. The court is talking. Everyone is whispering into someone's ear.

"Order! Order!" Judge McCrary pounds his gavel and says. Alisa walks like a scarecrow more than a woman and all lop-sided at that. As she nears, Judge McCrary's heart sinks right through his guts. She's more purple than brown. Her left eye is swollen, she can barely see her way to the judge. Her face still bears congealed blood and her clothes are an utter mess.

"People of the state of California versus Alisa Hopkins," the sheriff announces. Slowly, Alisa makes her way to the front of the court.

"Ms. Hopkins, you have been charged with section 187-199 the California penal code for attempted murder. Do you wave further reading of the complaint and complete statement of rights?"

"I do," Alisa utters before her lawyer could tell her what to say.

"And do you wish to enter a different plea at this time?"

"No," Alisa answers.

"How do you plea?" Judge McCrary inquires.

"Not guilty, Your Honor." The court resumes its chatter as if everyone expected a different plea.

Before Patricia can chime in, Grier says, "I'd like to file a motion to suppress, Your Honor."

"On what grounds?" Judge McCrary questions.

"The confession taken from my client was improperly obtained. She was inside her home, self-medicating to ease her pain away. Getting a confession from a woman who's heavily medicated on LSD is a low blow even for the city."

"Objection Your Honor. Ms. Hopkins was in a clear state of mind during her confession," Patricia responds.

"Your Honor, my client's constitutional rights were violated. Ms. Patterson invited herself into my client's home, pretended to be her friend, and conned a bogus confession out of her while she was heavily medicated," Grier snaps back.

"Motion granted; verbal confession will be thrown out." Patricia's Chinese cut bang blows upwards as she heavily exhales.

"Thank you, Your Honor," Grier replies.

"Ms. Patterson, I don't want this to turn into a repeat of the previous nightmare trial. Ms. Hopkins is a tax paying citizen and I want her to be treated as such. No holes, no leaks. Are we clear?" Judge McCrary asks.

"Yes, we're clear." Patricia knows exactly where Judge McCrary is going with his statement. He wants her on her toes and ready to play. He, like every other court official, wants to see Alisa pay for her crime and knows the entire state of California is following the case. So, every move must be made by the books.

"You honor, my client will like to request bail, again? Since her incarceration, she's been repeatedly attacked because of the information leaked by the department."

"Your Honor, there was no information leaked by the department. The defendant is making this up."

"Did she make up the bruises as well?" Grier snapped back. Before Patricia could reply, Judge McCrary interrupted and responded to Grier.

"Bail set at one million dollars."

"Thank you, Your Honor," Grier replied. Patricia lets out a deep sigh after the judge bangs his gavel. *How could he give her a bond*, she thought as she packed up her suitcase.

Alisa spots her target. He is a tall man, rather pale, and obviously lonely. Alisa sends over the waitress and she hands him a wine card, with of course the cocktail list facing up, and says: "The young lady to my left said, get whatever you like." He doesn't bother to look back at Alisa, he felt her eyes burning him from a mile away and he doesn't bother looking down at the card either. Off the dome, he knows what drink he wants.

"I'll take a tunic on rocks," he says. When the thin, big booby waitress turns to the bartender, he's already opening a bottle, and putting it out beside a highball glass with one rock in it.

"Hold on to your tray at all times," the bartender says to the new waitress. "And watch the cork center. It's to keep stuff from sliding," she prances back over to the gentlemen, puts down the glass and pours, and then takes the bottle back, throwing it into the box under the bar. The waitress must walk pass her customer again to get to the restroom. Before she reaches her destination, he motions her to him.

"You're new here?" he says.

"Yes, sir... this is my first night... If you have to know, you're my first customer."

"What's your name? I don't see a tag."

"Joan."

"Joan. That's a pretty name," he says.

"Ooh, well thank you," her country accent doesn't fit the location. He can tell she's new to California. Maybe she's here to chase her dreams and needed a dead in job to keep the lights on. He slides her a fifty-dollar bill and then says to her, "Tell that fine young lady to meet me on the roof top in five minutes."

Joan's eyes glance over to Alisa. Smoothly, she scoops the money into her bra.

"Will do," she replies.

Fine as vintage wine, Achton is standing by a fireplace on the roof watching California's beauty when Alisa arrives. It's a cold windy night. There is no one else on the roof and barely anyone left in the bar. Alisa knows it's now or never before she loses the nerves to do it altogether. She decides to go through with the plans she has constructed over and over again in her mind. She isn't sure whether or not he will go for it. There haven't been any signals so far; glances, smiles, body language; nothing. If he isn't a willing participant, her plan can backfire. She crosses her fingers and goes for it anyway.

In deep thought, Achton sits by the fireplace, sipping on some expensive cognac. He didn't even hear Alisa come up. Once he sees her, she desperately wants to hurry back out the same way she came, but it's too late. It's now or never. He's drunk, vulnerable and most likely, horny.

He's startled to turn around and see Alisa standing there. He assumed hours ago; she wasn't coming up. He tells her, he thought she had left and she assures him, she wouldn't leave before she got what she wanted. Then a dead silence falls over as the DJ switches from one record to another. Alisa looks at him, he looks at her and she assumes he's got the point right away. If he didn't get it, he surely gets it when she removes her trench coat, letting it fall to the floor, revealing her nude body clad only in high heels.

There is a brief moment when she thinks he's going to curse at her, tell her to fuck off, threaten to call Patricia and make up some horrid lies. However, none of it happens that way. Instead, he gets up from the fireplace hearth and walks over to her. The looks of astonishment on his face turns to lust as he makes the first move, saving Alisa the trouble. As soon as he begins to kiss her his phone rings. He silences it, knowing it's Chelsey just calling to check on him. Then, right after a second phone of his rings. He silences it too.

"You must be a very important man, to have two phones ringing off the chain," Alisa says.

"No, not really. I still carry my wife's phone with me," he replies before continuing his quest. He kisses Alisa very lovingly, like she's an old lover from high school who had just returned to their hometown. Alisa pulls the graphic biker t-shirt he's wearing up over his head, removing it and letting her hands gain the freedom to explore his massive chest. She sucks his bottom lip into her mouth while clawing her fingers down his chest. Their kisses gain momentum as he picks her up and carries her over to the bench.

There are no words, and both of them like it that way because neither of them knew what to say. Alisa's goal is clear-cut, but once Achton laid his hands on her, the benefits from her plan become appreciated. Her body is begging to be touched all in the right places. She's yearning for his touch. He lays on top of her, presses her arms up over her head and begins to drown her with his sweet kisses. As he moves down to her neck and then her breasts, she holds onto the end of the seat with both hands. Now, her hard nipples are prominent and manageable to suck.

He licks around her breast, starting from the bottom and going all the way to the top like he is licking an ice cream cone. His tongue is nothing short of magical as he uses the tip of it to trace a line down the center of her stomach to her belly button. Alisa pulls Achton's head back up to hers, after letting go of the seat because she yearns for more of his passionate kisses. She caresses his dick, feeling it grow to massive proportions as they both moan with delight. Alisa grabs Achton's ass cheeks, one in each hand,

and helps guide his dick inside of her hot, awaiting pussy. It welcomes him with much enthusiasm.

With one hand, Alisa holds onto an ass cheek and retakes hold of the wooden bench with the other while he fucks her harder and harder. While they look each other in the eyes, Alisa slips her hand from under the bench and grabs hold to Monroe's phone. She smoothly slides it across the floor near her trench coat and then resumes her love making.

She never expected the sex to be so passionate. She assumed she and Achton would have a rough little quickie, and then she would leave and go about her business after fifteen minutes or so. Instead, she and Achton go for what felt like hours on the abandon rooftop. For the fourth time, he cums inside of her. The flow of hot cum shoots up her pussy, causing a chain reaction. She comes a few seconds later. On top of her, he rests for a moment, both of them breathing heavy and savoring the fruit of their labor. When reality finally sets in, Alisa jumps up from the bench and grabs her coat. The look on her face is one of guilt, confusion, and happiness. Like Cinderella, she dashes out the door, down the staircase and out the bar.

CHAPTER 9

Patricia laid in Jason's arms hearing the rapid beat of his heart after she'd just finished sucking him to a blissful end. She's happy she brought him to his brink of pleasure since most times when she sucks him, he refuses to climax, always wanting to get inside her to reach his pinnacle. She finds it extremely gratifying to bring him to a level of exploding without him even entering her. He prefers to cum inside her pussy than her mouth. He doesn't understand the fulfillment she gets from pleasuring him orally.

She had to do something. Her hormones were high, and Jason was sleep, and she figured the quickest way she could satisfy her needs, is waking Jason up with a little head. It's been close to two weeks since Jason and Patricia has done anything sexually. The only thing they do is kiss when Jason is on his way out the door for work. As fine as Jason is and as horny as he stays, Patricia can't understand why he isn't interested in having sex more. In her eyes, they are pre-newlywed. They should be getting it on every chance they get and some. They should be at that stage where is hard to keep their hands off one another.

"You okay?" Jason asks tenderly.

"I'm okay. Why do you ask?"

"Because you look distracted and you are not saying anything."

"What am I supposed to say, baby?"

"I don't know. I just wanted to make sure you are good. You seem troubled by something."

Jason is absolutely right. Patricia is troubled by a couple of thoughts, like where he went the night she was almost attacked, or why his balls were sagging instead of tight. He hadn't been with her in two weeks, so they should've been firmer than a couple of stress balls when she sucked him to a bliss but saying this makes her the nagging bitter, black or ghetto, whichever one fitted the moment, woman. Patricia didn't want to be the one to start yet another argument between them. She wished like hell that Jason would start one off. That way she could get her point across and not be the villain.

Badly, she wants to bring herself to express to him her feelings. In the darkness, he can't see her ugly expression. As much as Patricia would love to think things are okay with them, she honestly didn't feel good about them at all. They have great careers, and are embarking on a new journey, for the most part, they're living an amazing life, but for her, she feels like the sex isn't where it should be. Patricia still can't get over the fact that she can't reach over and touch him in the middle of the night without him jumping up and acting like he wanted to attack her. The first time he reacted like that, it scared the life out of Patricia. She didn't think wanting to hold your fiancé was a bad thing, but from his reaction, evidently it is. He explained that she frightened him, but he always has the same reaction when she tries to touch him.

A few of the times he got mad at her for waking him. What man didn't want to be awakened by his woman holding his dick in her hand, ready to please him?

Patricia has asked him about her reaction to her touching him in the middle of the night, and he basically brushed it off like he always does heavy subjects. He assures her it's no big deal, but Patricia knows better. She can clearly see it's a big deal. The one thing about being his friend first and now his fiancé is that she can see when something is up with him. Why he wasn't telling her, bothered her. *Maybe I'm overreacting*, she thought. She tended to read too much into things sometimes. Besides the minor incidents and the decrease in their sexual activities, Jason isn't acting different. He's working more but Patricia knows he loves his job like she loves hers.

At home, he talks and laughs like he always does, but Patricia knows there is something he isn't telling her, and that fact irritates her a little. Patricia wonders if them getting married is a mistake. She loves him, but she loves their friendship more. It's so effortless. Marriage clearly makes things more complicated. The excitement of the wedding is still present but how long will it last?

"Where did you go that night I was almost attacked?" She goes against her gut and asks.

"I had to go clear my mind. That shit had me heated. I was thinking about going over to that bitch's house and fucking her up." In the back of Patricia's mind, she's thinking, *but Alisa wasn't home, she was arrested.*

"So, you just drove around all night?" Jason's story isn't adding up to Patricia and she silently prays Jason hasn't concluded she isn't the woman for him after all.

"Damn, Patricia! You just find anything to be mad about, don't you?"

"Who's mad? I'm just asking a question," Patricia tries to keep her cool.

"I'm not going there with you today, Patricia. I'm not trying to mess up my day before it even begins. You need to worry about this damn woman, who already made bail. You know you can't afford to lose another case against her," Patricia jumps up from Jason's chest.

"You know what, you only do shit like this when you're in the wrong."

"Wrong about what, woman? What have I done? Nothing."

"So, you say. If you've done nothing, why can't you answer simple questions without raising your voice? You have green veins popping out your neck, and for what? Because I asked you a question?"

Their voices rise above the sacred silence. One simple small question stirs a hurricane of harsh insults. Each of their Pandora's boxes open, sending words full speed ahead to shatter each other souls into a million pieces. His face brightened, just a tone lighter than her crimson. This is no longer "A mature adult conversation." Blood is bound to be spilled; feelings hurt.

"This is why you can't get ahead on this case. You focused on other bullshit. I'm starting to believe that you are not ready to work with *The Hawk*. I don't believe you are as qualified as I assumed," Jason has easily turned the entire conversation around.

"You think you are so much better than me, when in reality you're just a little momma's boy. You little wimp!" The worst thing Patricia can call Jason is a mother's boy. He has been teased all his life about being a momma's boy. His ex-co-worker Russel made it very clear that he had only made partner because of his momma's connects. Soon after, Jason quit the firm his mother got him a job at and applied for a job with *The Hawk*. He wanted to be taken serious. Patricia's words just set him back three-steps mentally.

"You fucking ghetto ass bitch!" his words are like daggers. They stab Patricia right in the heart.

"I'm sick of going through this shit with you!" Patricia wants to cry as rage fills her belly. She feels her ears getting hot. She scowls at him then spat out, "HOW DARE YOU?"

He sneers at her then laughs only adding fuel to her wrath. "Oh, you think your disrespectful ass insults are funny?" She snaps. He glares at her with hatred in his cruel dull eyes.

"You are an extremely angry girl. Aren't you?"

Their heated quarrel continues. It's definitely a war of words and who can hurt the other one worse. Both of them at each other's throats like savage hungry dogs fighting over dominance. When Patricia is out of words, she chunks the nightstand lamp at Jason's head. He's quick. He manages to dodge the lamp and the shoes that are being tossed his way. Furious that she misses her mark, Patricia charges at Jason.

She grunts as she takes a handful of his ass and attempts to wrestle him to the bed. Then she uses her free hand to start jabbing at his ribs. Jason takes Patricia by her hair, bringing her face down sharply onto his bent knee. Before he knows it, he pounds her head into his knee cap.

"Shit!" he blurts at his actions.

"I'm sorry, Patricia. I'm sorry," he says. He attempts to hole her, but she jerks away from him.

"You just put your hands on me, you bastard!" His heart sinks at the sound of her crack voice. Blood flows from her nose and as she staggers to the restroom. She locks herself in the bathroom until she is all cleaned up. And just like that, their little scuffle is over. For twenty minutes, they walk around the house in silence. No one is speaking. Then out of thin air, LAPD knocks on their door. It's no secret why. Jason already knew it had to be their nosey neighbor who called them.

His heart is pounding out of his chest. He's secretly praying that Patricia won't send him to jail. It could ruin his entire career and his mother would be so disappointed. But like a good wife, Patricia keeps quiet. She assures the police that noticeable damage was from an accident and that nothing is wrong with her.

CHAPTER 10

"I'm going to break this door down if you don't come and open it!" Patricia yells.

"It's open, trick!" Nichole yells back as she heads on out to the backyard. And I hope you are ready to watch a movie this time, and not be all glued to that damn phone."

"Oh, be quiet Nichole," Patricia says, coming through the double doors that lead to the deck.

"I'm turning my phone off tonight. What can I do to help?"

"Don't ask questions you don't want answers to," Jamellah says after Patricia passes her in the kitchen. Nichole is putting money-green sheets on the bed her husband built. It looks like something out of a movie. It's very clear that they are uppity California residents. Patricia or Jamellah has never seen a bed in a backyard. At least not one you'll want to sleep in. What Patricia and Jamellah don't know is, Nichole hasn't as much as sat on it since she's been living alone.

"Who'd you get all dressed up for?" Jamellah questions Patricia.

"This the dress you picked out for me at our new favorite boutique. Thirty-nine bucks. I had to remind Jason he got a hot chick with brains rocking his ring."

"It's nothing wrong with that," Nichole says.

"Oh yeah, now I remember. You're talking about the store that has everything under forty bucks? Oh yeah, that is my new favorite store." Jamellah replies.

Patricia nods. Both Nichole and Patricia both know Jamellah can't pass up a good deal.

"Did it come in any other colors? I can't do purple," Jamellah says.

"Yeah, white and orange remember. But they didn't come in a size skinny bitches."

"Damn!" the girls burst into laughter in unison.

"Why don't you make those tacos and shut up." Jamellah says. Patricia obeys, heading over to the bar where Nichole has all the fixings ready and waiting. Balanced high on top of a cabinet, the flat-screen TV awaits. Jamellah has already slid Love & Basketball into the DVD player. It's the only movie the girls agreed could never get old. No matter how many times you see it. Jamellah starts the movie and the previews start playing.

"What's the longest you've gone without sex?" Patricia asks Jamellah.

"I don't know. Two, three days, tops. Why?" Jamellah confirms Patricia's theory. Two, three days is the longest couples go without sex.

"Even after being together for seven years?" Patricia asks.

"Yeah. I have to have mine and Q is the same way. Why you ask?" Jamellah says.

"Because me and Jason got into a big argument last night and I mean it got ugly." Jamellah turns her full body around to Patricia.

"What happened?"

"I just don't think we have sex as much as we should and when I touch him at night, he jumps like a man in prison." Instantly, Patricia regrets spilling her business. She wishes she can take it back but it's too late now.

"Oh girl, a lot of men do that. They have a phobia about being touched at night. That's just their paranoia." Patricia doesn't say it, but she feels a lot better and somewhat guilty starting the argument off a hunch.

"I have to have mine every day!" Nichole yells from the deck.

"Really? I would have taken you for one of those snobby bitches who only wants it once a month," Jamellah jokes. Jamellah is right. Nichole is the type of chick who only wants sex once a month. It's part of the reason her husband is sleeping around with half of California, but she can't tell the girls that. She's used to being the girlfriend with her shit together. The perfect little housewife with the bubbly personality.

"Ha, ha, ha! I'm human, and just like any other woman, I got sexual needs to," Nichole says on her way into the kitchen with the girls.

"So, are you and Jason good in the bedroom?" Nichole asks sitting in one of the stools at the island.

"I mean, he's going to have to pick up the stamina to keep up with me for a lifetime. I'm like a diabetic, I need my sugar." The girls laugh endlessly at Patricia's joke. She'd rather joke on herself than admit to her girls that her man might be losing interest in her.

"I feel you girl. That is something you want to get straightened out before you jump that broom," Jamellah adds.

After a long night of jokes and laughter, Patricia isn't sure why she was tripping on Jason so hard in the first place. After hearing the girls talk about their problems and the things they've gone through with their men, she concludes that their problems aren't that bad. Patricia goes home feeling like a new woman. She no longer wants to slice Jason's head off, but she does want to suck the other one off.

V
B

Up the driveway struts the most perfect figure Patricia has ever seen. She couldn't tell if the girl is coming for the interview or if she had the wrong house. Her dimples are deep, she smiles a little as she spots Patricia waiting in the door for her. Her eyes are slanted like she has Chinese in her blood somewhere, but her caramel complexion tells otherwise.

She's definitely African American. Her hair is jet black, shoulder length and it blows with the breeze as she struts up the driveway. Despite the warm day, Patricia can't help but notice her cold sweaty hands. She extends her hand, "Patricia Patterson, Head lady in charge," she returns the gesture and shakes Patricia's hand with the gentlest squeeze. She speaks with the voice of one who's innocent and shy.

"Robin Martin, pleased to meet you, Ma'am," she smiles in the way girls do when they're masking nervousness.

"Well, you're early," Patricia says.

"Yes, I had to catch the bus and I hate to be late," Robin says. *Perfect*, Patricia thinks. *Someone who feels the same as me about tardiness.*

Within the first twenty minutes, Patricia decides Robin is hired but she informs Robin of the news after she prepares Jason's dinner. Robin answers every question perfectly. She's a shy spirit but she's very firm at the same time. Her cooking skills win Patricia over plus she can tell Robin will be a good maid. She has a daughter to provide for and a child is always good motivation to get the job done.

Out of all the men Patricia has dated, Jason is the only one that matters. He's her best friend, work partner and role-model at times. However, he's too damn sexy for words and she sometimes wonders how a heavy-set girl like herself ended up with him. In some ways, she feels as though she doesn't deserve such a quality man, and in others she feels like she does. Jason has been ignoring her since the fight, even though he is the one who was wrong.

Patricia has come to the conclusion his behavior is attributed to one of two things. Either he doesn't feel as strongly about her as he did when they first met, or he is sleeping around on her again. Maybe with his neighbor or maybe one of those groupie chicks from the firm. She strongly believe the problem is he isn't into her the way he used to be because if he were cheating, he would accuse her of cheating like he's done in the pass. That's how men do it, Patricia thinks. They accuse you of doing the same shit they are doing, in an effort to throw you off track.

Whatever it is, Patricia loves Jason, so she is willing to fake the funk, like she is happy, until things are back on track. She fell in love with Jason the first time she laid eyes on him, even though she had a slight concussion. Patricia met Jason when he hit her over the head with a hard baseball at a charity game. She was one of the cheerleaders, and he was playing first base. She remembers the game going smoothly, they were winning three to one. Next thing she knows, she sees the baseball heading towards her, and before she could duck, she was out. When she woke up, Jason was looking her directly in the eyes with a look of concern all over his face.

"Are you okay?" he asked.

"Hell, no, I'm not okay! You hit me with a damn baseball!"

That was it. The rest is history. They started working together on cases, then dating, then fucking, and now they're on their way down the aisle. Patricia refuses to throw away her happily-ever-after over some bimbo chicks.

When Jason comes home, he is greeted with a home cooked meal. He's unaware Patricia didn't cook the meal, and he's very pleased. Robin cooking was perfect, far better than Jason last maid. Patricia was able to pretend she cooked for her man without him knowing because the new maid listened to her versus the last maid Patricia fired, who only took orders from Jason.

The two talk about work for a little minute and then they dive into apologies right after. Jason assures Patricia he's sorry and feels less of a man for what he did to her and he promises to never put his hands on her again. Like a couple of high school love birds, the two make sweet love all night long and for the moment, Patricia isn't pretending to be happy. She *is* happy.

CHAPTER 11

A
chton arrives back home from chauffeuring Chelsey and her girlfriends around, totally exhausted, but he has no intention of breaking his date with Alisa. He had been thinking of her none stop after the bar and when she called him, he was too happy to see she had been thinking of him as well. He takes a long, hot shower that helps refresh his aching bones, shaves his facial hair, and transforms himself into a sexy bachelor by the time Alisa arrives to pick him up.

When she pulls up in her shiny black Maybach, he is anxiously waiting for her on the porch. It takes every inch of willpower in his body to keep himself from bum-rushing Alisa. Instead, he walks cool to the car with his head high. Deep down, Achton knows, it's way too early to be dating and definitely, with someone Monroe considered an enemy but every time he thinks of Monroe with Dawson, his guilt fades away.

As soon as Achton enters the car, Alisa hands him a dozen long-stemmed red roses, a box of candy, and a teddy bear holding a little red pillow that had *Be My Valentine* embroidered on it.

"I didn't realize the day I asked you to meet up with me was Valentine's Day, and leap year at that," Alisa jokes.

"So, I got you a little something. I hope you don't mind?" Achton is extremely impressed Alisa would shower him with so many gifts, having just met him.

"This is very thoughtful of you. Now I'm embarrassed because I didn't get you anything," he says.

"It's okay. You get a pass this year. Women are expected to cater to the man on leap year."

"Well, thank you again. But I still got to make it up to you," Achton says. One look at Achton's face and Alisa can tell he's in awe of her. Today she isn't dressed in a jail jumpsuit or a trench coat for that matter but instead a form-fitting, knee-length, red, bandage dress with nude Louboutin pumps.

They drive downtown, and Alisa surprises Achton with a horse-and-buggy carriage ride through Central Park. It's so romantic. Achton can't remember Monroe ever treating him to such a special event. Little does he know; the night is far from over. They spend the entire carriage ride getting to know each other better. Alisa tells him about her troubled up-bringing in Africa and how she's traveled the world and Achton tells Alisa about his poor upbringing in NYC. It's obvious they come from two different backgrounds but being poor is something they have in common.

After the carriage ride, they go back to the car and head to a restaurant/jazz club. Achton heard the place was nice but he never actually got to visit it. The restaurant is known for their steaks and true enough, they're good. So is the champagne. The band is fresh and their playing some awesome jazz music.

What Alisa doesn't know is, Achton is a die-hard Jazz fan and he once before Chelsey was born played in a band. He takes her totally off guard, when gets up from the table and goes on stage to sit in with the band. The members are some guys he knows from back in the day. He shakes hands with a couple of the fellows. One of them hands him a saxophone. He announces to the audience that he is dedicating his sax solo to Alisa. She can't help but blush. Dawson has never done something so bold and sweet for her.

Achton plays the saxophone with such grace and perfection, it makes her heart skip a beat like it did when he first touched her body. It's so refreshing to find someone who shares a love for music. Unintentionally, it makes Alisa's interest and admiration grow for Achton. *After I'm done with him, I just might keep him around,* she thinks. When he finishes his solo, the audience gives him a standing ovation. She stands up and claps louder than any of the rest. She even sticks her pinkies in the corners of her mouth, trying to get off a whistle or two.

They kick it way into the late-night hours, sipping more champagne, listening to the band, and delving deep into each other's mind. Alisa lets Achton know that she is scared to be nice to men because of past experiences and he's bent out of shape, trying to figure out how someone who ever want to hurt a person with such a loving heart. Then, he answers his own question. Most men can have it all and still want more. Well, he isn't like those men and makes it very clear to Alisa that he would never hurt her like the men in her past. His words are comforting to Alisa. She now knows, she has Achton right where she wants him. *In her web.*

It's getting near closing time, Alisa is quite tipsy, which makes her bold enough to talk freaky to Achton. She tells him, "I want you to take me someplace and fuck me in all three holes 'til I pass the hell out!" Astonishment comes over Achton's face. He recovers quickly, Alisa quickly pays for the check. But instead of leaving the club like Alisa thought they were, Achton lead Alisa through the kitchen and up a stairwell. The club is on a street level of a large building. Achton knew of its spots through internet reviews, plus he has friends who have talked about the restaurant more than once.

They walk up a good four flights, Alisa has no idea where Achton is taking her, but she's all for the surprises. She likes the boldness in Achton. He stops at the top of one flight of stairs and starts unlatching a window. He pushes the window up, and the February air starts breezing in. He helps her out on to the fire escape. It's a little difficult because of her tight dress.

Alisa warns Achton of her fear of heights and he assures her, nothing will happen to her. Once he kisses her, all of her fear disappears, and she becomes lost in his touch. His kisses are so tender, his hands are so gentle, and her pussy is incredibly wet. She starts to unbuckle his belt while he begins to work on her dress, pulling it up and exposing first her thighs and then her black satin panties. She got his pants unzipped and finally whips out his dick. She tells him to sit down on the steps of the fire escape. She sits on the step directly below him.

She starts sucking his dick, immediately she partakes some of his delicious precum. It makes her want to suck it all in and that is exactly what she does. She deep-throats his entire average size penis until his balls are slamming up against her chin as she takes it in and out her warm mouth. He leans back on his elbows and enjoys being her late-night dessert. She pulls his pants down farther around his knees and spread his legs, biting gently on his kneecaps as she works her way up to his balls. She carefully takes his balls sack into her mouth and then suckles on it, contracting her cheek muscles around it.

Alisa sucks Achton long and hard. It's been awhile since she's had a dick in her mouth, and it feels good. She has never sucked a white boy before and that mixed with the excitement of being on a fire escape, turns her on even more. She sucks Achton royally, she needs to be sure he will never tell her no, whenever she asks for something. He sprays his babies down her throat. She continues to suck his soft dick until he is hard again. To her, they still have some unfinished pleasure to attend to.

Once he is hard again, he gets up and tells her, "Get on your knees on the step and spread your legs," Alisa complies and pushes her booty out to meet him as he rubs the head of his white and pink dick up and down her ass crack. She's craving him to take her ass because his dick just isn't big enough to get the job done from the front. But of course, he moves his dick just where she doesn't want it, her pussy.

"No, the ass!" she says. He complies and thrust his dick into her ass, and she is dazed. His dick was perfect for her ass, unlike Dawson. His dick was too big. Achton starts fucking Alisa hard, just the way she loves it, and then spread her ass cheeks so he can finger-fuck her pussy at the same time. Before he can push his fingers all the way in her vagina, she begins to cum all over his hands. The two are in a bliss. For her, then him. *What a night?* They thought as they dressed themselves.

CHAPTER 12

The scene is quite unbelievable, shocking really. Patricia's mind is sent reeling, unable to comprehend or process the images that's being sent by her eyes. She looks away, then looks back to see if it's still there. It is. An office full of roses. Patricia's training kicks in, she's trained to deal with this kind of foolishness.

"Rebecca, come get rid of these flowers for me love."

"What would you like me to do with them?" The temp secretary trails Patricia closely into her office.

"Well. You can do whatever you like with them, sweetheart. Just get them out of my office," Patricia takes the card from the Dom Perignon and it reads, *It's a celebration Kiddo, don't drink it all in one night.*

"Here, enjoy." Rebecca's eyes buck wide. She's undecided on how to take Patricia's kindness. *Is this a test,* she thinks as she slowly takes the bottle from Patricia's hand.

"What would you like me to do with this, Ms. Patterson?" Patricia looks the temp in her eyes. She looks to be no older than twenty-one, twenty-two maybe at the most.

"I'm sure you can figure that out," Patricia says before flopping down into the cushioned leather chair. Alisa's games are starting to get to her. Her words haunt Patricia's mind, making her move with a lack of confidence. Over the last couple of months, Patricia has become familiar with Alisa's ghost moves. Her puzzle statements echo repeatedly, sometimes in Patricia's dreams and sometimes out the blue during a normal working day. Her tactics control Patricia's every move.

The power of her strategy is beginning to tear down walls it's taken Patricia years to build. But no matter the price of the challenge, Patricia want quit. It's not in her nature to. Patricia turns her chair in a three-sixty and now she's facing the floor to ceiling mirror on the closet door. She stares at herself, or at least the inaccurate image of herself. The mirror shows her the woman the world sees. A woman who makes moves like fireworks, who's ambitious, and very confident. Somehow it doesn't match the woman on the inside. Inside, she's scared, shy and nervous.

She looks deep into her wet brown eyes and says to herself, "You got this, Patricia. You are a force to be reckoned with. You have witnesses, a bullet, motive, and the law on your side." Suddenly Patricia feels optimistic. You can turn off all the lights and still there is a flame in Patricia's soul, always burning for victory, always ready to start a new blaze. She closes her eyes and enjoys the positive flow, recharging her neurons until they rekindle and spark.

"I am great. I'm the shit. I will nail this case and become the best damn lawyer in LA. I am everlasting fire. My hope will never be extinguished before my earthly time is done." Patricia rocks back and forth in her chair, chanting her pep-talk with her eyes closed.

"Did you say something, Ms. Patterson?" Rebecca barges into the office and asks. Her presences startles Patricia, she opens her eyes, sits straight up and says, "I have to make a run. Forward all my important calls to my phone."

"Yes, ma'am."

Patricia exhales. She didn't even realize she was holding her breath. She jumps up from her chair and grabs her black leather Chanel bag on the way out.

B

Patricia's first impression of the Goslings was good will. Chelsey seemed to be a normal teen girl who believed everything her parents did was done to ruin her life. And Achton seemed to be a good loving house husband, at least that was the first-time Patricia saw him. His attitude was the complete opposite the last time she saw him. Achton was a complete and utter mess. Tears, anger, and emptiness are only a couple of words Patricia could use to describe him.

Patricia expects to feel the same vibe when she arrives at the Gosling house; sadness, anger, frustration. Chelsey's last wish to Patricia; *get her for this*.

Instead of that sad vibe, Patricia gets a completely different vibe; one of joy and happiness. Chelsey is so caught up on her new gadgets; she doesn't even bother asking her how she's coming along on nailing her mother's killer. Achton, who could barely stand or breathe, is now bouncing around like a new man. He's glowing, energetic and hopeful for the future.

"Me and Chelsey are going to Hawaii in a couple of weeks. When will you need us to testify?" *Doesn't matter when, this is your wife*, Patricia thinks.

"It'll be soon, but in the meantime Mr. Gosling I'm going to need you and little Ms. Chelsey to stay put," Patricia says. "We still have a lot of work ahead of us, if we want to put the woman who did this away. I mean she's throwing some crazy accusations out there."

"I mean, what if you're looking at the wrong person?" Chelsey says.

"Well, if she didn't do it, it looking really bad for your mother. She's claiming that your mother is the murderer and I'm pretty sure she has evidence and motives to back up her accusation." *Wow, how attitudes have changed*, Patricia thinks as she scoops up her bag from the coffee stand.

"How can you be so sure?"

"Sweetheart, a woman like Alisa doesn't purchase bread and not use it." Chelsey stands confused.

"I hope that we're still on the same page here, because if the family doesn't care about clearing their loved one's name or care to find her murderer, then I'm in deeper shit than I assumed." That familiar anger resurfaces on Achton's face.

"Chelsey, I'm going to walk Ms. Patterson out. I'll be back to whip on you in a few. And don't cheat!" Achton says, pointing to the *Sorry* board game.

"Listen, I don't need you or anybody else for that matter, coming around here trying to make my daughter and I feel bad for wanting to move on with our lives. Monroe has done enough damage to this family. Yes, we love her, yes, we miss her and yes, we want her name cleared of this mess. But put your feet in our shoes. I don't know what to believe anymore. My daughter doesn't even know what to believe anymore. For all we know, this Alisa could be telling the truth. What kind of people would be, if we placed an innocent woman behind bars for a murder she didn't commit?" Patricia snatches her arm away from Achton's tight grip aggressively.

"Are you saying Monroe may have committed the murder, Achton?"

"I'm saying, I don't know who did. I'm saying it's not me or my daughter's job to find out. That's kind of what you get paid to do. You know, to put murderers behind bars and free the innocent." Achton's words sink in more than Patricia leads on.

"Just be ready to testify when I call you. You're not to go anywhere until then," Patricia snaps before strutting off. As soon as she is buckled into her car her phone rings.

"Hey baby," she says at the sound of Jason's voice, "Hello."

"What you doing?" Jason asks.

"I'm leaving the Goslings' home. I needed to check on them and ask a couple of questions. Can you believe they were planning to take a vacation to Hawaii? I mean, like we're not gearing up for a trial."

"It's good thing you went over there, then."

"Yeah, I know."

"They're probably just really stressed and trying to find a way to deal with it."

"Yeah, maybe you're right. Listen, baby I'm going to pull an all-nighter. I got a lot I need to go over tonight. I'm heading back to the office as we speak. You think you can manage without me tonight?"

"Yeah, baby. I understand. I might be doing the same depending on how things go here," Jason replies.

"Okay, baby. I love you. I'll see you when I get home."

"Okay, I love you to baby. Make sure you eat something and don't work too hard," Jason says.

"I won't. Bye."

CHAPTER 13

J ason is sitting all alone by the fireplace in the living room when Robin arrives. It's a little chilly outside; windy night. Robin uses the key Patricia keeps under the welcome mat by the garage door to let herself in. She knew Jason would be alone. Patricia called her from work earlier in the day and told her she will be working late.

Robin knows it's now or never before she loses the nerve to do it altogether. Hesitantly, she decides to go through with the original plan she's been paid to do. She isn't sure whether or not Jason will go for it. There has been signals here and there; glances, smiles, body language; but she still isn't sure. If he isn't a willing participant, her plan will never work. She crosses her fingers and goes in anyway.

There he is sitting by the fireplace, sipping on some expensive cognac, and listening to classical music; his favorite. He doesn't even hear her come in. Once she sees him, she starts to hurry back out the same way she came, but she remembers it's either now or never. So, she speaks, "Hello, Jason," he's startled to turn around and see Robin standing there.

"I used the spare key; I hope you don't mind. I let myself in."

"No. It's fine, but Patricia is at work. She'll be working overtime," Jason says.

"Oh, that's fine. I'm not here to see her. I'm here to see you," she says.

"Is something wrong?" Jason asks.

"No, not at all." A dead silence falls over the room as one CD track ends and another begins. She looks at him, he looks at her. Robin thinks he's gotten the point right away. If he didn't get then, she's sure he got gets it when she unzips her good girl maid costume, letting it fall to the floor, revealing her nude body garbed only in high heels.

There is a moment when she thinks he's going to turn her down, put her out and threaten to fire her, but he doesn't. Instead, he gets up from the sofa and walks over to her with his dick poking out his pants. There is a look of lust written all over his face. His heart is pounding, he can hardly wait to have Robin wrapped in his arms. He's being silently watching her from a far, for a while now. Not because he wants to love her for a lifetime or leave his woman, but because her beauty is just breathtaking.

He would never leave Patricia for a woman like Robin because he knew better. Patricia is everything a real man wants in a woman; smart, loving and he doesn't have to worry about her running around on him in the streets, but Robin is everything his body craves. She looks like an urban model who just walked out of King magazine. He's honored that she's been watching him, just as much as he's being watching her. He can barely believe that he's kissing her, that she's now wrapped in his arms. He kisses her very lovingly, like an old lover who has just returned from overseas. He and Robin knew nothing about one another. Only that they were craving each other's touch. She pulls the cable-knit sweater he is wearing up over his head, removing it and letting her hands gain the freedom to his massive chest. She sucks his bottom lip into her mouth and digs her fingers into his chest.

Their kisses gain momentum as he picks her up and carries her up the stairwell to the master bedroom, their bedroom. Once inside, he lays her on their bed, and Robin watches as he removes his jeans and silk boxers.

"You're so beautiful," he says. Robin lies still with her heart beating out of her chest. She's over with, if Patricia walks in on them fucking in her bed.

"What do you want? Jason asks.

"I want you, anyway you want me," Robin says.

"In that case, turn over on your stomach." She obeys his orders, turning over on her stomach. She can already tell where he's going with this. He leaves the bedroom for a few seconds to retrieve a bottle of lubricant from the master bedroom. Upon his return, he takes his fingers and rubs it all up and down her ass and his dick. He fingers fucks her ass for a few minutes, to judge her reaction and figure out whether anal sex is her sort of thing or not. Robin moans with pleasure, so he knows the deal.

As she lay there on her stomach with his dick grinding in and out her ass, screaming and holding onto the headboard for dear life, she wonders what Patricia would say at the very moment if she walked in. Robin prays she doesn't have to find out. That is not part of the plan. She needs the money from the job and she actually likes Patricia, but business is business, and she needs all the money she can get right now. Her daughter is her first priority and money is all the system respects.

He explodes in her ass. It's a wonderful feeling. She takes his dick out of her ass and jumps up from the bed. He's in heaven, and very tired. Robin was everything he imagined her to be; a beast in bed. Her blissful love sends him right to sleep. On his stomach, he's snoring like a baby.

"Damn, that was quick," she whispers before pulling the hidden camera out of Patricia's Valentine's Day teddy bear. Jason was mad easy, Robin concludes. He isn't half the guy she expected him to be. He seemed to be a guy with morals and business about himself. But like every other dog ass nigga, pussy weakened him. Robin has cameras all over the house, but she knew if she got through to Jason, he would be so doggish that Patricia's room would be the first place he would take her. It's like the ugliest betrayal feels the best to men.

She pockets the camera and dashes out the door. The last thing she need is for Patricia to catch her. She would then be out of a job and wouldn't get paid for the side job. Alisa means business and the deal is *don't get caught.*

CHAPTER 14

The whole idea of a swinger party is strange from the start, but Alisa promised herself that once she hit forty, she was going to take the sexual-prime theory to heart and let go of all her inhibitions. However, Dawson was never down for the adventure; which is strange to Alisa because he couldn't seem to keep his dick in his pants during their entire marriage. Maybe he wanted her all to himself, or maybe he wanted to seem like a decent man to her. Whatever his reason for not wanting to be adventurous in bed was, it slowed Alisa down on her journey and now that he is dead, she is ready to get on the prowl again.

Achton and Alisa arrive at Achton's old buddy's house about midnight. People in wild-ass costumes and masks are everywhere. Alisa is wearing a black leather cat outfit with a tail and snaps in the crotch, with no underwear underneath. It's strapless and has a push-up bra built in, so her perky twenty-something looking breasts are looking delicious. There is a leather whip that comes with her uniform. Instead of wearing it in its place, on her hip Achton is holding it to keep her in line.

He's sporting the Phantom of the Opera costume, with a black tuxedo and cape on, along with a white mask. He spots his old friend and tells Alisa to make herself comfortable; he'll be back.

After downing a couple of Long Island ice teas and watching people dance and get intimate with each other in the designated dancing area, Alisa decides to accomplish the task on hand; to get kinky, very publicly. She takes a quick survey of the area and spots Achton surrounded by a couple of his friends.

She walks over to him as confident as Naomi on a runway. She clears her throat and gets ready to use the Spanish accent she practiced.

"You look like a walking dream," she whispers into his ear.

"Damn, do I know you sexy?" Achton jokes looking Alisa up and down.

"Not yet, but you're about to get to know me." Alisa reaches down and starts caressing Achton's dick through his pants while his friends look on with envy.

They holler out typical macho things like, "Damn she's bad man," "Punish that pussy man," "She about to work you, man."

"Naw, I got this, bro," Achton says. He starts palming her ass and other guests from the party start looking on as well, including the group of women Alisa overheard talking about getting Achton. They are instantly jealous.

"What do you have in mind?" Achton says. Alisa pushes him down on a chair at one of the round tables covered with black linen tablecloths and then straddles herself over his legs, facing him.

"Let me show you what I have in mind." Alisa wants to pat herself on the back because her Spanish accent is so bomb. She sticks her tongue deep inside his hungry and waiting mouth. He gladly returns the kisses, and right off the bat, Alisa knows she's going to enjoy fucking the life out of Achton in front of his friends.

After they tongue the hell out of each other for about three minutes, she stands up between his legs as she lowers the front of her leather suit, allowing her perfect breasts to be viewed by everyone in the room. Miraculously, a silence befell the room, and the only sound that remains is the music. Absurdly, it is "Sex me," by R Kelly. Everyone is in awe. Alisa glances over at the group of girls, who are in a daze, before she decides to hold her left breast out for Achton to suckle on.

He eagerly takes her hard nipple into his mouth and fed off it like an infant on its mother. Then he decides he wants them both, he grabs a hold of each one, and rapidly moves his head and tongue back and forth from left to right. Alisa's pussy is getting so wet from all the excitement that she begins to care less and less about who's watching. She felt like her identity is safe behind the mask and new wig.

Panting and moaning, they fuck each other like beasts until they both explode in unison. The night is bigger than any fantasy Achton has ever had. He walks out the party feeling like *the* man.

"I know how we started dating is weird, but I'm really honored to know you. You've been a dream in the flesh. I've been happier with you these last couple of weeks than I have been with Monroe our entire marriage." Good sex always leads to good pillow talk. Alisa lays silent on Achton's chest. She listens closely as he pours his heart out.

"When you told me, you weren't the killer. I was mad because I knew it was a possibility that Monroe could be. I mean I've never said she did it without evidence, but I do know how her temper is. That night I told myself over and over, she wouldn't do anything so horrific, but the truth is, I'm not sure what Monroe is capable of. It's like I've been married to a stranger all these years."

"She seemed to have a bad temper. Did you ever have any problems with her getting physical with you?" Alisa asks and like a man facing a life sentence, Achton begins to spill.

"Yeah, I mean she and I fought all the time, but just typical husband and wife stuff, you know? Nothing as serious as murder."

"Yeah, I know what you mean. I couldn't believe half the stuff I found out about Dawson. I feel so stupid and used." Alisa's tears rain on cue. It's like she's auditioning for the highest paid gig in Hollywood.

"You not stupid, Alisa. We were just in love. What happened to us can happen to anyone. But we can't allow their mistake to affect our lives."

"That's easy for you to say. You're not fighting for your freedom, I am."
Instantly, Achton feels guilty. Alisa jumps up from his bear hug and
searches for her clothes

"Wait a minute, Alisa. Don't go, talk to me," Alisa continues to clothe
her body.

"I'm sorry, that was inconsiderate of me. Talk to me, I'm here for you.
You don't have to shut me out."

"How are you here for me, Achton? No one is trying to help me. You
got what you wanted, so just leave me alone," she cries out as she quickly
zips her dress up over her curves.

"I'm not like your husband or the other men in your life. Alisa, that's
not me. It's not who I am. If I say I'm here for you, that's what I mean."
Achton grabs Alisa by the hand, then pulls her close to him so that she
cannot go anywhere.

"How can I help you, Alisa?" Achton doesn't know how sweet his words
sound to Alisa. On the inside, she's smiling. She stares at the floor with her
wet eyes for a good ten to twenty seconds and then hesitantly answers,
"Can you testify about you and Monroe's domestic disputes?" Achton pulls
away from Alisa and flops onto the bed.

"See, I knew it. You're just like all the others. Everyone got their hand
and dick out, but nobody is offering anything," she resumes dressing
herself.

"I didn't say I wouldn't help, Alisa."

"Yeah, and you didn't say you will either, did you?" Silence sweeps the
room.

"Exactly, you're not trying to help me. All I'm asking for you to do is
tell the freaking truth and you can't even do that!" Achton knows Alisa is
right. She deserves a fair chance at justice and she'll never get that if he
doesn't testify because police stick up for police. He's seen it done more
times than one to know. Alisa looks at Achton's guilty face out of her

peripheral view. She can tell he's almost caught in her web, so she takes one more jab at it.

"It's okay; you don't have to help me. I'm sorry for even asking. I'll see you around." She scoops up her crocodile Hermes bag from the nightstand.

"You didn't ask me for anything, Alisa. I volunteered and I want to help you and I will. My word is my bond. You can count on me." Achton wraps Alisa up in his arms as she cries her eyes out on his shoulder.

CHAPTER 15

"Do you swear to tell the truth, the whole truth and nothing but the truth so help you God?" Jose shakes as he places his hand on the Bible for his oath. Will his testimony help or fry the woman who's been so good to him over the years? Will God applaud him or condemn him for his lack of loyalty? *God, surely understands*, he thinks.

He raises his eyes to look at Alisa. She smirks at him and then nods her head. His testimony can easily be the testament that puts her away, but what choice does he have? If God didn't understand, surely, Alisa understands Jose is only doing what he is told. His voice is small as he recites the oath. He drops his eyes to the dusty planks of the courtroom floor.

"Mr. Willis on Wednesday, October fifteenth you called the 9-1-1 operator. What did you tell the dispatcher, exactly?" The clicking of Patricia's heels echoes throughout the courtroom as she paces back and forth with her hands pressed together in front of her mid-section.

"I told them that there were shots being fired inside of the Hopkins' home." Jose's heart is pounding, and his lips are trembling. He's never been on a witness stand and the pressure is slowly giving him anxiety.

"Were the shots just inside the Hopkins' home or did some of them get fired outside as well?"

"There was one shot inside of the Hopkins' home. When I heard it, I ran to see if Ms. Hopkins was okay."

"What did you do to see if she was okay or not?" Patricia asks.

"I beat down the door until I heard a gun shot being fired out the window. Then I ran off to call for help."

"Question, how many shots did you hear that day, Mr. Willis?"

"I believe it was one."

"Was Mr. Hopkins alive before detective Gosling arrived on the scene?" Patricia picks up an honorable picture of Monroe from her desk and holds it up so that Jose can see, and then the jury.

"Yes." The court room breaks into chatter. Patricia is on to something. The energy in her stride across the court room is becoming noticeable.

"Yes what, Mr. Willis?"

"Yes, Mr. Hopkins was alive when detective Gosling arrived on the scene."

"How would you know if he were alive or dead? Was you in the house at the time?" Patricia rephrases her question to see if Jose will change his answer.

"So, you are telling the people of the court that Mr. Hopkins was alive the day detective Gosling arrived at the Hopkins house, on Wednesday, October 15?"

"Yes, Mr. Hopkins was alive but he was already shot." Jose answers. I know this because the gun shot went off before Gosling arrived and when the ambulance comes out the house the only person who was on the stretcher shot was Mr. Hopkins, so that led me to believe that Mrs. Hopkins shot Mr. Hopkins.

"Was there any gun shots going off after Detective Gosling arrived?"

"No, there weren't any more shots that I remember." "When was the last time you saw Mr. Hopkins alive?" Patricia asks.

"I saw Mr. Hopkins arrive home a little before he was shot." Shamefully, Jose looks over to Alisa and then holds his head down. He feels less of a man as he fries the woman who has fed his family for many years. If the jury cared any, he would tell them that Dawson got everything he deserved. For years, he had been using Alisa and cheating on her. It was no secret. The entire staff knew about it. The maids and butler would talk about it daily.

"What's a little before he arrived, an hour, thirty minutes, ten minutes, what?" Patricia didn't let up. She can sense the hesitance with Jose's every answer, but she didn't care. Her victory counted on his testimony.

"I'll say maybe thirty minutes, maybe forty at the most."

"I have no further questions, Your Honor." Patricia struts to her seat, takes a sip from her glass of water and then watches proudly as Alisa's lawyer takes the floor.

"Mr. Willis?" Kelly Robertson one of the three lawyers Alisa has on her team struts her stuff confidently to the witness stand.

"Can you tell the court the first time you ever saw detective Gosling?"

"It was Wednesday around twelve or maybe one o'clock that afternoon." A loud disturbing growl from Jose's stomach sounds throughout the courtroom. He's so nervous he can shit his pants. The Caucasian lawyer places her hands over Jose's shaking hands to soothe his nerves.

"It's okay, Mr. Gardener. You're going to be fine. Just answer the questions as truthfully as you can, and we can get this over with." Jose nods while staring deeply into the blonde's blue eyes.

"Now, was this the same Wednesday Mr. Hopkins was shot?"

"Yes," Jose manages to answer through all the quivering.

"Objection, Your Honor!" Patricia blurts out.

"The witness just said he didn't see Mrs. Gosling until she arrived on the scene after the 9-1-1 call."

"You Honor, the witness simply answered Ms. Patterson's question, which was that he witnessed Dawson arriving home thirty to forty minutes before he was shot, and that Mrs. Gosling arrived on the scene after the 9-1-1 call. He never said that was his first-time seeing Ms. Gosling."

"Objection overruled," Judge Brown says. Patricia takes the punches like a woman. She rolls her eyes at the blonde and then flops back into her chair.

"So, let me rephrase this for the court. Did you see detective Monroe before she arrived on the crime scene the day Mr. Dawson Hopkins was killed, Mr. Willis?"

"Yes. She visited the mansion earlier that day."

"What did Mrs. Gosling want when she arrived to the Hopkins mansion, exactly?"

"She was looking for someone. She demanded I tell her where they were, but I told her I didn't know what she was talking about. I was scared she may hurt Ms. Hopkins so I told her no one was home."

"Why were you scared of Mrs. Gosling? She's a detective; an officer of the court?" Kelly asks.

"At the time, I didn't know she was an officer of the court. She wasn't dressed in any uniform. I was scared because she had me pinned down at gun point."

The courtroom breaks into chattering, slipping out of the Judges control. He bangs his gavel and says, "Order! Order! I will have order in my court room!" As soon as the court is quite again Kelly resumes her questioning.

"Can you tell the court what kind of gun Mrs. Gosling pointed at you?"

"She aimed a .45 at me, a black .45." Stunned, Patricia drops her head to the desk. Deep down, she's now wondering if Monroe truly is the killer.

"When Mr. Hopkins arrived that day, thirty minutes before he was killed. Did you actually see his face, or did you just see his car?" Patricia exhales aggressively, she wants to object to the phrasing of the question, but she's more eager to know Jose's answer.

"I knew it was him because it was his car, but I didn't see his face because the windows were tinted," Jose replies.

"Did you see him get out the car?"

"No, he drove the car into the garage and entered into the house through the garage."

"So, let me make this clear. You didn't see Mr. Hopkins driving his car; you didn't see if Mr. Hopkins got out his car, so there is no way you can honestly tell the court that Mr. Hopkins was shot or not when Mrs. Gosling arrived to the Hopkins mansion for the second time on Wednesday, October 15."

"Correct," Jose blurts proudly. His testimony isn't all bad, he thinks. Maybe there is a chance he can help save Ms. Hopkins, after all.

"So, Mrs. Gosling could have been driving Dawson Hopkins' car and you wouldn't know, would you?"

"Objection, Your Honor. Come on?" Patricia jumps on her feet and yells out.

"Objection sustained. Mr. Willis don't answer that. The jury will disregard that last question."

"I have no further questions Your Honor." Kelly does a three-sixty spin, turning from the witness stand to Alisa's direction in her four-inch heels, then struts back to her seat. The court is chattering again, this time louder. People are whispering in their neighbor's ears. Confused, Chelsey and

Achton remains silent in the court room. They don't know what to believe. Every day they discover something new about Monroe's secret life.

Flipping through her witness papers, Patricia is fed up. If it wasn't for her reputation she would throw her hands up on the case.

"This is all a game," Patricia mumbles.

"I'm sorry, did you say something Ms. Patterson?" The Judge asks.

"Yes! I said this is all a game to her. The witness never mentioned that he had any prior engagements with Mrs. Gosling."

"Yes, because you never asked," Ms. Clarkson blurts back.

"The court is going to take a recess. We will continue tomorrow morning at eight," Judge Brown bangs his gavel and frees the court room.

"Yes, Your Honor," Patricia replies before gathering up her things. Heading out the court room, Patricia doesn't take one look at Alisa. She doesn't want to give her the satisfaction. She struts out with her head held high looking forward to the exit.

CHAPTER 16

Alisa: *I want to feel you inside me.*

Achton: *I want to be inside of you.*

Alisa: *Let's meet at your place. Get rid of the kid! Hehehe*

Achton: *I'm dropping her off in the woods as we speak. I'll be waiting on you.*

Alisa: *Good. I want you blind folded. I need to release some stress.*

Achton: *Stop it girl! You got me losing it.*

Alisa: *I'll see you in a flash*

Achton: *I hope so.*

When Alisa arrives to Achton's home, a few blocks from the courthouse, she's determined to get the job done on hand, and dip. Things were panning out in court for her, but she has a couple of kinks that she must iron out.

She knocks on the door and slides it open. She peeks inside, sees no one, and decides to let herself in. The house is quiet and there is no Achton in sight. She makes her way back to he and Monroe's room thinking, *this is perfect*. When she reaches the master suite, still there is no one in sight.

She reaches for her purse to pull out the letters and instantly she gets a slight sense of fear in her heart. She feels she's being watched, so she doesn't pull out the letters. Instead, she scopes out her surroundings once more and there on the nightstand sits a chilled bottle of champagne, some flute glasses, a dozen roses and a blindfold. *Damn, he's easy*, she thinks as she flops onto the bed.

Alisa drinks some of the champagne. It's nice and cold. Afterwards, she sits on the edge of the bed with the blindfold in her hand waiting for Achton to reveal himself. She knows he isn't far. She just wishes he would come out already. She didn't plan on spending her entire day with him. A little after her drinking her first glass, she hears footsteps approaching the room from the hallway. She can hear Achton whistling as he enters the door.

"Stop right there!" Alisa demands. Achton is startled by the toughness of her voice. He stops in his footsteps with his hands held high.

"Now turn around. Put your hands behind your back." Achton's adrenaline is charged. He's enjoying every second of this moment. Alisa walks up behind him, spreads his legs with hers and then blindfolds him until he sees nothing. She begins to strip him of his clothes.

"Help me. The quicker you're naked the better," Alisa whispers into Achton's ear.

"What happens if I don't help you?" Achton asks.

"Umm, I got a bad boy on my hands I see." Achton can feel Alisa walking away from him. His heart is pounding. He doesn't know what to expect.

"Let's see," Alisa takes one look at Achton and sure enough he is still blindfolded with his hands behind his back. She eases out the letters from her purse and then opens the nightstand drawer. She slides them in so smoothly, Achton doesn't hear a thing. Afterwards, she closes the drawer back on the nightstand, Patricia looks over to the left of her and there is one of Achton's thick leather belts.

"Perfect," she blurts out. Achton's heartbeat increases at the sound of her voice. He's so busy trying to figure out what it is she's found he's not prepared for the whip that strikes him on the ass.

"Ouch!" he blurts out.

"Now, what was I saying? Oh, yeah. I want you on your knees. Crawl to me, and beg for my mercy." Slowly, Achton drops down to his knees and begins crawling towards Alisa like a slave obeying his master.

"Umm, I like. I like," Alisa utters out as she watches him slowly approach her. She moans at the sight of his beautifully cut body. Just as he gets closer to the bed, they hear a loud outburst from Chelsey and her friends. The girls are giggling and heading towards the bedroom.

"Oh, shit! Fuck. Dammit." Quickly, Achton blindly runs to the door to lock it.

"Daddy, are you in there?" Chelsey yells as she beats on the door.

"Yes, give me a minute Chelsey. I'll be out."

"Okay." Achton is beyond pissed but Alisa isn't. She can barely catch her breath. She's laughing with her hands covering her mouth.

"I'll sneak out the Jack and Jill bathroom and then slide out the side door. That way her friends won't know I'm here," Alisa says.

"That sounds good," Achton whispers before Alisa slips through the bathroom and out the side door. Ten minutes into her drive she gets a text from Achton.

Achton: *This is not over yet!*

Alisa: *You been saved by the bell…. Heheheh*

Achton: *I always hated school.*

Alisa: *lol.. Catch up with you later…. Bye!*

CHAPTER 17

Patricia knew her girls were throwing her a party the night before she jumps the broom, but she could've never prepared for this night. Jamellah and Nichole went all out for her bachelorette party. After the rehearsal dinner, she assumed they were going to take her back to Nichole's house and have a stripper or something. She couldn't have been farther from the target.

Instead of taking Patricia to Nichole's house, they drove about an hour out the city to what appears to be an abandoned warehouse. However, there are tons of cars outside and people walking in and out the front doors, mostly women from both of Patricia's jobs.

When Patricia enters the warehouse, it's the freakiest shit she's ever seen before. Dick for days! She's been to her share of strip shows but she's never been to one where all the men were dancing butt-booty-naked. There is no sign on the door, but once inside, there are neon signs everywhere with the club's name, *The Fountain of Youth*, on them. Patricia, Jamellah and Nichole join the other girls who had beat them to the club at the tables in the back. All the tables in the front had long been taken. Patricia greets all of her friends whom she hasn't seen since the wedding planning process had begun. Her sisters are even in attendance looking like two ghetto fabulous hood queens.

"We're going to keep this show Rated PG ladies!" Patricia does a three-sixty spin in the floor pointing to all her girls at the tables. She sits down and the fit muscular waiter comes to take their drink orders. He's fine as wine and the girls are lusting all over him. They're acting like men in a strip club.

"Did it hurt?" Jamellah yells out to the waiter.

"Did what hurt, baby?"

"When you fell from heaven." The girls start howling at Mr. Sexy. They're beyond ready for the night ahead.

"I would love to lick a Pina Colada off your ass!" Loretta screams out to the waiter. Patricia giggles at the girl's behavior. She tries her best not to join The Girls Behaving Badly club. Although, it's very hard to do when there are big, juicy dicks dangling all over the place.

A few minutes later Mr. Sexy returns with the ladies first round of drinks. All while another fine-ass guy is sitting in Jamellah's lap blowing in her ear; she is Patricia's maid of honor. Patricia is speechless; she never even knew the place existed. It's an underground freak show. The Fountain of Youth is huge. It's a warehouse turned into a big-ass fuck palace. *Sex Me* by R Kelly kicks in and another sexy hotshot takes center stage and begins to do some of the most amazing acrobatic fuck moves the girls have ever seen. The way he is pretending to grind his dick in a vagina makes the girls scream for him.

"You betta work!" one model looking female screams out from the front row.

"Girl, do you see how long his tongue is?" Nichole murmurs to Patricia. She just nods in astonishment. He continues to grind his dick seductively until the song ends. When *Lost Y'all Mind* by Kilo Ali comes on next, he gets buck-wild.

The girls are torn up by the third round of drinks, and by the fifth round, they're all horny. Patricia is silently wishing she could get her hands-on Jason right now, while she is steaming. She would fuck him like she hated him. There is a competition going on between the men and the women but there is no one to judge who is wilder. The male dancers are freaky, but the girls seem to be a little freakier. There are some freaky things going on in The Fountain of Youth.

There are some men who have women bent over tables, grinding their dicks up against their asses, they are palming tits, sucking toes, and even fingering pussies. As for the women, they are worse. The women are pulling the men's clothes and accessories off too, jacking penis', riding dicks with their clothes on; everything except actual fucking.

As much as Patricia loves the show, she realizes it's getting late and she's ready to get home. She knows Jason must be worry that she's out past two a.m.

"Thank y'all for a good night but it's getting late and I should be getting home before I don't have a man to go home to." Patricia stands and stretches for the stars.

"Oh, the party isn't over yet, honey," Jamellah says. She then calls over one of the sexiest men in the room and whispers something into his ear. Patricia sits back in her chair. She's more nervous than a murderer on trial. She assumes that Jamellah is telling the young man to come over and turn her world upside down. That scares her because, so far she's managed to keep her hands to herself, in a room full of temptation. Five minutes later, the waiter returns with other waiters and a cake. While their waiter sat the cake, which is chocolate and shaped like a huge dick, on the table, the other three clapped and recited some rehearsed congrats-on-your-wedding verse. Patricia is relieved that the cake is the surprise and instantly she loosens up a bit.

Her relief turns to panic when the finest guy in the place comes up to her. The man is hitting. He's six-foot-five, two-hundred-ten or two-hundred-fifteen pounds, chocolate-skin, with jet-black curly hair and deep brown eyes. He stands out in the club because he has on clothes; a pair of fitted Levi jeans, a suede vest and of course some cowboy boots. He leans over the table, reaches for Patricia's hand, and she almost faints. At least that's how she feels.

"You betta get your ass up girl!" Nichole yells out.

"What the fuck is going on?" she mumbles to Nichole.

"Just a little something extra I have planned for you! This is your last night of freedom. Now, GET THE FUCK UP!" Nichole says. You can tell from the expression on her face that she can barely prevent herself from breaking out into a full grin. Patricia is drunk, and his hand is still reaching out for her. Hesitantly, she takes his hand.

A couple of minutes later, he and Patricia walk through a set of double doors in the rear of The Fountain of Youth. He has yet to say a word to her. She figures Jamellah has paid him to give her a private dance, sort of like a male lap dance. She's still very nervous. If he had just been an average cute or even remotely fine, she wouldn't be so nervous. The problem is, he passed all those, and he is abnormally fine. Her vagina is throbbing, and her heart is racing and he's only holding her hand. She has a gut feeling that she should turn around before she gets herself in some serious trouble once he finishes his little freak show. She should have stopped him right then. She should tell him how she is feeling uncomfortable and how she would like to rejoin her friends so they can leave. But she doesn't, and before she knows it, they reach their final destination.

There is a long hallway in the back of the club with several rooms. All the rooms have neon signs over the doorways. He leads her to one called, *The Red Light Special* and holds the door open for Patricia to go in. The room is dimly lit with red lightbulbs, and there is a slow jam playing. There are three couches in the room, each one on a wall, and two of them are occupied. Patricia tries to pull her hand loose after she sees what is going on in the room but he holds onto it tightly and speaks to her for the first time, "Don't run away, baby. At least let me do my dance for you. Don't worry about them."

He has the deepest, sexiest voice, and when he looks at Patricia with those bedroom eyes, Patricia is at his beck and call. So, Patricia obeys and doesn't worry about them. She goes and sits on the couch the farthest from the door while he walks over to the compact shelf stereo system and changes the CD. There is absolutely no dancing going on, and when

Patricia's private dancer goes to put on his performance music, Patricia can hear the others moaning, fucking, and sucking noises.

One girl is over on the sofa by the door, and her ankles were pressed up over her shoulders while a big, mandingo-looking brother is fucking the life out of her. The other is not quite as bad. However, she is sitting on the couch on the left wall sucking another man's dick like a popsicle on a hot day. Apparently, the lap dances they received were enticing because they are all about fucking.

After all sorts of shit starts going through Patricia mind faster than the speed of light. She knows she should be thinking about her baby, Jason, her husband-to-be, but he never crosses her mind. The worse part about it is, she doesn't even feel guilty. He's cheated on her before and she's no fool. She knows what goes on at bachelor parties. *His ass probably fucking some hoochie now*, she thinks as he puts on his music.

The man fucks Patricia every which way but upside down. If time permitted, they probably would have gotten to that position eventually. Patricia needs about three days to fuck him the right way. Instead, they only had about three hours, but they made good use of them, though, and he tore her vagina up. He gives her a whole new meaning to the phrase "dick whipped."

When she rejoins her friends, after quite some time, they are about the only ones left in the entire club. Some of the girls have left already. Those remaining are the ones she's riding with, including Nichole and Jamellah. They are both grinning and laughing at her. She doesn't even attempt to fake the funk because there is no way they will have believe she's been back there talking for the past three hours plus.

She does the next best thing and tells them all about it on the way home in the car, blow by blow, and they are all ears, envisioning every second of it.

CHAPTER 18

T he first-time Jason laid eyes on Robin; he knew that he wanted to feel her insides. The first time he kissed her, he thought he would explode in flames. He promised himself that he wouldn't touch her again. The risk is too high. He loves Patricia and can't imagine the pain he'll experience if she should ever find out about his betrayal and leave him. But the closer he and Patricia's wedding gets, the more he's eager to get the bad boy behavior out his system.

Jason is home early from work and Patricia is at the office. He decides it's the best time to seduce Robin one last time. He figures if he doesn't quench his thirst now, he can possibly ruin his marriage because it'll just be on his mind until he does. He knows his body cannot settle down for another night's sleep without Robin. She invades his every thought. He dreams of her doing things to him all the time, whether he's stuck in traffic or working. The mere thought of her doing things to him that Patricia is against makes him stiffen.

Jason's eyes are glued to Robin's butt. It's moving side-to-side as she dries the dishes. She's a fantasy in the flesh. Quietly, Jason makes his way into the kitchen. He sneaks up behind Robin, pressing his hardened penis against her butt.

"Where's my wedding gift?" he whispers into her ear.

"You're not married yet," she replies with a sheepish smirk.

"I want to feel your insides." Robin turns around to face Jason. She's biting down on her bottom lip as if she's heard the best news all year. She takes her hand and slowly trails it to his midsection. There, his penis is standing at attention, poking out his slacks.

"How long have you been dreaming of this moment?" Robin asks as she unzips his pants.

"Since the last time you touched me," he's staring blankly into Robin's eyes. He wants nothing more than to be inside the walls of her anus but this time he wants more time to actually enjoy the ride.

"Its that so?" Robin lets go of Jason's pants and they drop to the floor. She takes her hands and rubs them up and down his back; underneath his shirt. The anticipation of her every move is killing him. She sticks her head under his shirt and begins to trace a trail with her tongue around each one of his nipples and down the middle of his chest to his belly button. She gets down on her knees and licks each one of his thighs and then turns him around. She takes the thickness of her tongue, licks the entire crease of his ass, and then sticks her tongue deep inside his asshole. Just as she assumed, he's into the freakiest shit. Most men in his position were.

She can feel him shiver as she turns him around again and takes his balls gently into her mouth, suckling them softly. Robin devours every inch of Jason while he stands there and dick-feeds her. He runs his fingers through her bob while shoving more of his penis into her mouth with each slurp. Robin can taste his pre-cum and before he can explode she jumps up. He tosses her onto the counter and thrust his dick deep into her. The initial thrust is painful but in a pleasurable way. Robin moans out, "Aww, shit! Fuck me Jason, fuck me," her words are too much for him to handle, he can feel himself cumming, so he pulls back a little. When it's safe, he dives back in. Pounding at her cake, neither of the two realizes there's an active phone call on Robin's phone. Her buttocks accidently dialed a number.

"Girl, you're going to make me do something to your ass. Shit!" Alisa listens attentively to Robin and Jason until she's had enough.

"Mommy!" Riley screams through the phone. Alisa figured the sound of Riley's voice would get her attention before she could, plus she doesn't want to blow her cover.

"Mommy, are you there?" Robin pulls up from the counter a little and sure enough it's her phone she hears the noises from.

"Hold on, wait." Jason digs deeper into Robin's guts, assuming she's finally feeling the pressure.

"Stop, dammit! Wait!" she yells pushing him away from her.

"What? What's going on?" Robin throws her hand up to hush Jason up.

"Hello?" Robin blurts into her phone.

"Hey mommy," Riley says.

"Riley?" Alisa snatches the phone from Riley.

"I hope you're not over there falling in love and shit. Business and pleasure never works out," Alisa says.

"Did you forget you had a visitation scheduled at my house today?" Robin quickly jumps off the countertop and pulls her skirt down.

"Shit! I'm on the way," Robin never answers Jason suspicions, she just runs out the door.

B

"What happened to her?" Patricia's voice startles Jason when she prances into the kitchen. Timely, he just tucked his penis in and zipped up his pants.

"What you say?" he stutters.

"I said, why did she run out of here like that?" Jason can barely breathe. He's so nervous, he's almost sure Patricia notices it.

"Oh, I don't know. She got some phone call and just took off. The only thing she said is '*I got to go*'." Jason wipes the countertop off with the dish rag for the fifth time. Patricia can barely breathe from all the bleach he's spraying. He busies himself, cleaning off the stove after the countertop. A quick glance at Patricia and he assumes she's piecing things together in her head.

"Why are you cleaning up Jason? You don't ever do any cleaning?" Patricia is coughing, trying to fight off the strong fumes.

"Jason, stop with the bleach before you kill me. And get out my kitchen! That's my damn dish rag you wiping the stove off with."

"Well, excuse me for trying to help," he jokes, snapping his fingers like a gay man.

"Robin will take care of it when she returns, or I'll do it. You just get out my damn kitchen." Patricia's words are heavenly to Jason. The quicker he can get out of her presence the safer he'll be.

"Why are you home anyway?" he asks on his way out the kitchen.

"I needed to pick up some things. Plus, I'm hungry," she answers.

"Do you want to grab something to eat?" Jason asks.

"No, I really don't have the time to go and eat. I'll just warm up the leftovers in the refrigerator." Jason silently exhales, he's relieved. He doesn't want to be around Patricia right now anyway. He's afraid she might smell his guilt or Robin all over him.

"Well, I got to get back to the office myself. I'll call you later. Maybe we'll have time to go for dinner," he says before disappearing out the house.

CHAPTER 19

The moment Patricia slides into her chair she's served an enormous platter of food. Eggs, ham, piles of fried potatoes. A tureen of fruit sits in ice to keep it chilled. The basket of rolls Jason sits before her can keep a homeless family going for a week. And there's an elegant glass of orange juice, that Patricia wastes no time gulping down.

"Somebody woke up on the right side of the bed this morning," Patricia says before she digs into the eggs.

"This is just bait to get you to marry me and then all bets are off." Both Robin and Patricia burst into laughter.

"On a serious note, I know you've been busy with the case and I just want you to get a fresh start this week. With the trial going on, and all."

"Aww, that is so sweet baby. Look at my man, being all supportive and everything," Patricia jokes.

"But baby, you forgot one thing…"

"What I forget, baby? Oh…. It's the bacon, right?"

"No Jason, I don't need more food. This is more than enough."

"Then, what is it woman?" Jason jokes.

"You forgot to thank Robin. Because I know you don't think I think you cooked all this food." Robin chuckles as she cleans the pots.

"Oh, I see what this is!"

"What, baby?"

"This is gain up on Jason day," Patricia burst back into laughter and then suddenly she hears her phone ringing from her bedroom. She takes another sip of orange juice and then jumps up from the table.

"Excuse me y'all, I have to get this," she says before dashing upstairs.

"What are you doing? No phones during breakfast baby, come on now."

"This won't take long baby, I promise!" she yells out. Jason looks out the kitchen into the hall to check if the coast is clear and when he sees there is no sign of Patricia, he turns to Robin and says, "So, what happened the other night…."

"Can never happen again…" Robin chimed in and said.

"I mean, you are one amazing, sexy, beautiful…shit! Let me stop before I get myself into some trouble but damn girl!" Jason briefly presses his manhood up against Robin's buttocks.

"If you walked into my life a little earlier, I would have my way with you." Robin can barely control her blushing. She is staring at Jason with googly eyes, giggling like a teenager with a crush. She enjoys Jason's compliments and lives for his admiration. The attention is addictive. She almost wants to take his penis out and kiss it for his kind words, but she knows better. It's like he said, if only they had crossed paths on a different note during a different time.

"What the hell going on in here?" Patricia brash voice startles Jason and Robin and they both jump like kids do when they've been caught with their hands in the cookie jar.

"What you talking about?" Jason stutters.

"I'm talking about you invading her private space and her giggling like she's flirting with LL Cool J." Everything in Patricia's gut tells her that the picture isn't innocence. She knows what flirting looks like and Robin and

Jason were definitely flirting. They're definitely feeling one another. And, why wouldn't they? she thinks. They are both finger-licking good.

"You taking it wrong, Patricia. It's nothing like that," Jason says.

"It's nothing like what, Jason? Why are you all in her personal space and shit? I mean shit, you're close enough to kiss. I bet she can smell my pussy on your breath you're so close." Robin is as silent as a mouse. She doesn't know what to do or say. Badly, she wants to run out the kitchen and never look back, but she needs her job.

"Patricia, stop it. You're embarrassing me and yourself," Jason says.

"Oh, I'm embarrassing myself? Am I? Why are you so close to her Jason? Answer that for me, and what you say that's so damn funny? She's looking at you biting down on her lip and shit!" Pressure is building up inside Patricia, her gut is tangled in a knot. She's like a ticking bomb, ready to explode. She wants to reach over and punch Robin in her face, but she knows the consequences and it's no way she can afford jail. Not with Alisa on her tail right now.

"Get out my house bitch before I beat you black and fucking blue." Robin steps a foot back from Patricia's fist. She can tell it's taking all the good in Patricia to keep from striking that blow. *Damn, I'm glad I got them damn tapes before this shit. Alisa would kill my ass.* Robin reflects on her way out the door.

"Really, Jason! My maid, Jason?" Patricia cries out as soon as Robin shuts the door behind her.

"I'm telling you, Patricia it's not what you think." Patricia throws her hand up at Jason's lie and then takes off upstairs to lock herself into her bedroom.

"Patricia! Patricia…. Open the door, please!" The sound of Patricia whimpering from the other side of the door cuts at Jason's heart. He beats on the door until his knuckles are raw, but Patricia gives him no answer. Loudly, she cries herself back to sleep.

Desperate, cold, and curious, Jason sits outside the bedroom door waiting on Patricia. He wants to be right there when she finally frees herself from the bedroom she's turned into a prison. Some odd hours later, Patricia appears out the bedroom. Jason's presence startles her, but she doesn't say a word. She takes a second to grip onto her beating heart and then she continues her quest to the kitchen. No words are passed between the two for the rest of the day. The two play hooky from work only to sit in silence at home.

CHAPTER 20

Slowly and reluctantly, Patricia uncovers her face. She blinks, closes her eyes, and blinks again. Streaks of sunlight stab through the window and blind her. She sits up and instantly, the fresh scent of the lilies attacks her nostrils. Jason isn't taking the cheat route with his begging. The room is full of flowers, chocolates, and *I'm sorry* balloons. Patricia looks around but there is no Jason in sight. She drags her feet off the bed and rubs her knuckles onto her eyes.

She then stretches her arms above her head and yawns. Bringing her arms back down to waist length, she notices there is a new, bigger, shinier ring on her finger.

No, this fool didn't buy me another ring, she thinks as her legs dangle above the off-white polyester carpet.

"I hope you like it," Jason says from the doorway. His voice startles Patricia. She jumps a little before her heart sets back to calm. Slowly, he walks over to the bed where she is sitting and flops down beside her. He and Patricia share a silent conversation as they stare blankly into each other's eyes. Patricia finally looks away, tears threatening to blur her vision. Gently, Jason takes her hand into his. It's soft and warm, reassuring almost.

"Patricia, I want you to promise me something," he whispers, his expression utterly serious.

"I know you're angry with me and I know your feelings for me may be a little wary but please promise me that you won't ever shut down on me like this again. No matter what it is we are going through. We are supposed to get through it together. I can take you cussing me out. Calling me names even but I can't take the silence. So, whatever it is, however you feel, just come out and say it. Let me know so I can fix it."

"I just feel like things are getting," she pauses, silently staring into the free space ahead of her, "Can we just talk about this later? I have to get ready for court and really can't afford this distraction right now."

"I understand that. We can talk about this over dinner tonight. I just want you to know that I love you."

"Do you really?" Patricia snaps. Jason's lips turns up into a tiny smile, it's good to hear Patricia's voice, even if she's not being nice with her words. He pulls her in closer to him, hugging her tightly to his chest.

"Yes, I do." he whispers, capturing his lips into a kiss that felt just right.

"Now, go kick ass," he says before Patricia disappears into the bathroom.

Finally, the day Alisa has been preparing for is here and there is no halting the time. Everything hinges on what she does today in court, and once done it can never be undone. She can barely think straight with everybody watching her. As she slowly walks to the witness stand she can feel the cold stares. It's as if they are staring a whole right through her soul. Most times when people look at one another like this, all love isn't only lost but transformed to a powerful hatred. Chelsey's eyes locks on the woman that has accused her mother of murder, but she feels nothing inside. No hatred, no hope, she's just blank. As Alisa drags over to the stand and takes her seat, she exhales roughly. The courtroom is a meaningless backdrop to her, a mere stage for the drama to come.

"Do you swear to tell the truth, the whole truth and nothing but the truth so help you God?" The Bible rattles as Alisa rests her shaking hand onto it for the oath. Her life depends on her testimony today. She has absolutely no room for mistakes.

"Hello Ms. Hopkins, how are you?" Kelly Robertson asks.

"I've been better," Alisa jokes but the only laughter in the court is her own.

"Do you recognize this lady?" Kelly flashes an honorable picture of Monroe in uniform.

"Can you tell the court who she is?"

"That is my late husband's, mistress," Alisa answers.

"What name did you know her by?" The clicking of Kelly's heels echoes throughout the courtroom as she paces back and forth.

"I knew her as Detective Monroe Gosling."

"So, you knew she was an officer?"

"Well yes, I asked for her specifically when I called 9-1-1, remember? But I didn't always know she was a police."

"But you knew at the time you called for help?" Patricia asks.

"Yes, I knew but I didn't always know."

"Okay Alisa, when did you learn Mrs. Gosling was an officer?" Alisa's facial expression is lifeless, not just sagged but lacking its usual liveliness completely. It's as if she's left her spirit back in her cell. Her eyelids droop, and there is a slight slouching to her head.

"When she asked me to kill my husband." Instantly, the court breaks out into chitter-chatter. Both Achton and Chelsey are curiously looking around, investigating the conversations around them.

Patricia's face falls faster than a corpse in cement boots. In that instant, her arms chill up, her mouth hangs with her lips slightly parted and her eyes are as wide as they can stretch. *This bitch*, she thinks. There isn't even a point in objecting. This is Alisa story and she's clearly sticking to it. She glances nervously into the court crowd looking for confidence. If they look hopeful then just maybe there is a chance, then all bets were on. But they don't, they only look surprised. They're in disbelief just as Patricia is that Alisa is really going through with her accusations.

"Why would she want Dawson dead?" Kelly asks Alisa.

"Monroe wanted Dawson to leave me for her, but he made it clear that he wasn't and after that she begins calling and texting all times of the night. When he asked her to back off, she became furious and that's when she told me she was a police and that I should think twice before I make a police mad." Cool wind blows from Patricia's mouth as she exhales with frustration. Today is turning into one of those days and she wished she was in bed at home watching a black and white movie.

"Did you kill your husband, Alisa?"

"No, I didn't kill my husband." On cue tears drips from Alisa pretty brown eyes. She's sobbing like she's some weak woman who needs a good friend.

"If you didn't kill your husband, who did?" Kelly is feeling really good about the case and the direction its taking. She's standing over by the jury box confidently waiting on Alisa to pull herself together.

"Monroe, killed my husband," Alisa finally utters out.

"But wasn't it your gun that killed Mr. Hopkins?" Kelly's voice increases, she knows her point is getting closer.

"No, it was Monroe's gun who killed my husband," Alisa takes the Kleenex from Kelly and dabs her dripping tears.

"Can you explain these texts between you and Monroe?" Kelly passes around a copy of the text printed on paper.

"Initially, she denied sleeping with my husband but then she went on to say that she wasn't the type to be played and how I was weak for letting my husband play me." Patricia reads the texts. She can't understand how Alisa got Monroe to hang herself with texts. If Alisa hadn't confessed to her the murder she would probably believe was innocent to. Patricia is almost certain that the jury is buying Alisa's bullshit.

"Thank you, Mrs. Hopkins. I have no further questions Your Honor." Kelly struts back to her seat like she's walking a runway.

"Your witness Ms. Patterson."

"How did Mrs. Gosling react when you told her that you weren't going to kill your husband?" Patricia is still sitting in her seat.

"She told me if I didn't kill Dawson that she would put the murder on me anyway. She said she knew people, important people in the right position to make it happen." Reading the documents in her hand, slowly, Patricia stands to her feet.

"Can you help me? I need better understanding. So, you say if you kill your husband, Detective Gosling promised to help you get off on his murder, right?"

"Yes, she was the brains behind the entire operation," Alisa answers confidently.

"But you went to jail and beat the murder case, correct?" Alisa's saliva builds up and she swallows hard. *This isn't looking good.*

"Yes," she murmurs.

"I'm sorry, I couldn't hear you. Did you say, yes?" Patricia is now standing directly in front of Alisa. From a far Jason is admiring her strategy.

"Yes," Alisa repeats.

"So, is it safe to say you killed your husband and detective Gosling helped you get off on the murder? You're not in jail right now because you took Mrs. Gosling up on her offer and you killed your husband? Detective Gosling was your accomplice, not your enemy?"

"Objection, Your Honor she's badgering the witness."

"Ms. Patterson!" Judge Brown blurts out.

"Okay, I'm sorry Your Honor," Patricia replies.

"Help me understand something Mrs. Hopkins. If Dawson is dead, you're are the accused murderer and detective Gosling is free, why would she kill herself?" The court is silent. In suspense, everyone is stiff as mannequins waiting on an answer. On the inside, Jason is screaming, clapping and congratulating Patricia. He's very proud of his woman at this very moment.

"Objection, Your Honor. Come on! That question is very misleading. How is she to know why Mrs. Gosling killed herself? That answer would be a matter of an opinion not evidence." Kelly stands to her feet to blurt out.

"Objection sustained. Ms. Patterson, I'm warning you." Patricia holds up her hand for peace.

"I have no further questions Your Honor."

"This court will recess and return Thursday morning at eight thirty." Judge Brown bangs his gavel and dismisses the court. Patiently, Jason waits for his superstar outside the court doors.

CHAPTER 21

The door left ajar cast a white beam into the sultry night. It's odd for a door to be left open in this part of town, as a rule they were shut, locked and double bolted. Burglars were always trying to break in the homes around the nicer neighborhoods. The robbers approach the door and call out.

"Is anyone home?" the female calls out with a disguise voice. There is no answer. The male robber pushes the door and it swings open with ease, a blast of cold air streams past him and some light jazz drifts from a room out of sight. There are a few items like magazines and DVDs cast onto the floor in a haphazard fashion but otherwise nothing of concern. Quietly, they ease into the townhome watching their every move.

"Close the door, damn!" the male robber whispers to his counterpart. A weird sound echoes from the back of the house and Mr. Bad Guy reaches for his weapon. Slowly he walks towards the noise with his eyes bucked wide. He checks behind every door and wall on his way back. He concludes there is nothing to see, his paranoia is just getting the best of him.

"Go ahead and do what it is you need to do." Quickly, the girl runs up the stairs and straight to the master bedroom. She didn't need a map; she knew her way around all too well. Quick and smooth, she rambles through the boxes on the top shelf in the closet and after three minutes she finds the treasure but it's not the kind of treasure that shines. Careful, she switches the .45 in the box with the .45 in her purse. Neatly, she stacks the boxes back onto the shelf and it's as if they have never been moved. Swiftly, she skips back downstairs, and she finds that her friend has ransacked the place. There is nothing in its place.

"Did you have to do all this?" she asks with her hands waving out at the mess before her.

"Shut the fuck up and look for some money, jewels, anything we can get some money off of."

"This wasn't part of the plan, man," she says before joining him in the treasure hunt.

"Did you do what you're supposed to?"

"Yeah, I did. We're good," she answers.

"You didn't see anything of value up there?" he asks as she tossed paintings off the walls, in search for a secret safe of some sort.

"No, I don't think we're going to find anything here. It doesn't look like a home that splurges on material things," her heart is beating faster than African drums and all she wants to do is leave.

"Yo, let's go. We don't know if there are alarms here or not," she says with fear in her voice.

"Man, chill. This not my first rodeo shawty. Look around for some money. I know it's got to be something around this bitch."

"Bye. I'm out!" Quickly, she dashes out the house and he's right behind her.

CHAPTER 22

Making love in unusual places has always turned Jason on. His desire is to be more creative when it comes to making love with Patricia. So, he decides to surprise her by planning something particularly special. He wants to do something completely different than the norm, to prove he's truly sorry for his behavior.

Jason spent a lot of time on a farm with his grandfather growing up and he often talks about how much he misses the days of his youth to Patricia. She's told him many times how his stories make her want to visit and he promised they would one day. One day had come quicker than Patricia anticipated it would.

It took quite a bit of preparing and a hell of a lot of negotiating to find someone who was willing to let Jason use their facilities, but he did. Jason found an older couple, who's still romantic at heart and gracious enough to let him carry out his plans on their property. He'd plan the whole day out when Patricia was mad with him. Finally, the moment has come for him to wow her and his nerves are a wreck.

He parks the car directly in front of a barn, letting the high beams highlight the barn doors so they can see how to enter. He tells Patricia to get out the car and she complies. He asks Patricia to close her eyes, takes her by the hand, and leads her inside the barn. Once inside, Jason tells Patricia to open her eyes. She's completely shocked to see a king-size bed adorned with huge, fluffy pillows and wildflowers wrapped up in ivy flowing around the bedposts. There is also a small bouquet of wildflowers sprawled across the bed, just for her.

There is a round table with a red linen tablecloth about twelve inches from the bed. The table has white torch candles burning on it and is set with fine china. A bottle of wine is chilling in a silver cooler, and Jason has a vase of wildflowers placed in the center of the table. The barn has four horses in two stalls on one side and six cows in stalls on the other side. They are pretty calm, doing what animals do, like eating hay, grass or whatever.

"Have a seat," Jason says to Patricia. He leaves for a moment to kill the headlights on the car. When he returns, he finds Patricia looking around in dismay from her seat at the table. Charmingly, Jason laughs at Patricia.

"They're just horses, they won't bite."

Patricia bursts into laughter. "I'm not scared of these horses, crazy. I'm just looking at them."

"Patricia?" Jason slowly walks up to Patricia and whispers into her ear.

"Yes, Jason."

"I love you, Patricia," he replies.

"I love you too, baby." On cue, the doors to the barn open up, and the violinist enters, wearing a black tuxedo. He starts playing for them, and instantly Patricia's heart begins to dance. A smile creeps up on her face. Patricia is really shocked when the waiter enters, also wearing a black tuxedo, pushing a rolling cart covered with a white tablecloth, the kind they use for room service in upper-crust hotels. The food is catered by a nearby sea-food shack.

"Baby, you really went all out," Patricia says as the waiter pours the wine.

"You were great in court baby. I feel proud to call you my woman."

"Is this what all this is for?" Patricia waves her hand out at the beautiful spread of food: the lobster in butter sauce, yellow rice, steamed vegetables, and buttered rolls.

"No, this is my way of saying sorry."

"Sorry?"

"Yes, sorry. I'm sorry for hurting you and not showing you how much I appreciate you. You've been very patient with me and understanding and I just want to return the favor for once." The two are quiet for long minutes while the violinist continues to play soft music.

"I know I haven't been the perfect man, but I want us to work. So, I'm trying to clean my act up before we marry. I know asking you to forgive me is a lot but, I'm doing it anyway. Patricia, will you forgive me for all of my bullshit?" *So, you do know, you've been bullshitting me around?* Patricia thinks as she takes a sip of the wine.

"Please?" he begs. *Oh, he begs*, she thinks. The silence is killing Jason. He continues to stuff his mouth trying to keep calm or at least look calm. *Oh, who am I to judge? I did do my little thing the other night*, Patricia sips more wine as she reflects on her bad girl behavior.

"I forgive you Jason and I want us to work just as you do," Patricia's words are like music to Jason's ears. He swallows his food down and before he can respond his phone goes off.

"I thought I turned this thing off," he says before answering.

"This is he... What! Fuck, okay…No, we are on our way."

Patricia sits in suspense waiting on Jason to end the call to say, "What happen? Who was that?"

"That was the home security. They say they've been trying to reach you." Quickly, Patricia digs in her purse for her phone that Jason had made her turn off earlier.

"Oh shit, they did call me!" she blurts.

"Our place has been robbed. We have to go!" Patricia stares deep into Jason's eyes for a long ten seconds. It's her place that's been robbed, he barely has anything there, at least not anything of value. She jumps up from the table in a rush and follows him out the door. *So much for a romantic evening*, she thinks on her way out.

When Patricia and Jason arrive at the house, they spot a light on inside and the door is ajar. Figuring the robbers just left the door opened behind them, they walk right in. It takes a few seconds for their brains to translate the image they see as reality. Their carefully ordered world has been systematically ransacked. The filing cabinet is opened, and the bookshelves lay bare, their previous contents in chaotic piles on the floor. Even the family portraits are roughly smashed into the floor, their frames ripped apart and photos tossed to one side. Whoever had been here was desperate to find something, but what? And would they come back?

Quickly, Patricia dashes upstairs to check her Lord-Have-Mercy money that she hides in her bathroom wall, Sure enough the entire fifty G's is there. Then she checks her safe for her gun and it's there as well.

"Whoever it was, they were some rookies. They didn't even know where to look for the good stuff." Jason walks in on Patricia as she's re-shelving her gun back on top of the shelf.

"Yeah, they had to be because they didn't find the money or the gun. They both are still here," Patricia says.

"I think it was that bitch just trying to scare you. I know I gave you hell in the past about this bitch, but I truly see now, she's a nut case," Jason says before walking over to Patricia to hold her.

"Let's just make a report and we'll stay at my place." Patricia nods her head and rest silently on Jason's chest, wrapped up in his arms until her shaking stops.

CHAPTER 23

"Honey, I was in such a rush to get ready for tonight, I completely forgot to put on my panties!" Achton grins as Alisa whispers into his ear. The valet pulls off with their car. They've just arrived at Alisa and Dawson's favorite restaurant, at a luxury hotel downtown. Alisa has rented out the entire revolving restaurant on the top level.

They enter the lobby of the hotel, and the bellman suggests they take the glass elevator up instead of the regular elevators in the center of the building. It's a beautiful night and the view of the city is magnificent. Both Achton and Alisa's eyes are glued to the view as they ascend to the fortieth floor. There are two other couples on the elevator with them, but they don't stop Alisa's show. She's standing behind Achton, and none of the others can see her hands. She lifts the back of Achton's dinner jacket and starts feeling on his ass. He jumps a little at first, startled that she would do such a thing.

Achton was used to being conservative in public with Monroe but Alisa is a different kind of fun. She knew exactly how to hit his spots. The couples drop off the elevator before they reach the top. When they walk into the rooftop restaurant, the maître d' greets them with a large smile.

"Your seat is right this way." The maître d' says.

"We must be a little early? Where is everyone?" Alisa gives Achton a devilish smile and then follows the maître d' to the table.

"You are so full of surprises," Achton mumbles as he follows close behind. While the dinner is being prepared Achton and Alisa order drinks to get the night started. Alisa orders a Pina colada, and Achton orders a Cîroc and orange juice. When the drinks arrive, Alisa takes the cherry out her drink and pops it into her mouth. Attentively, Achton watches her as she twirls the cherry in her mouth. Alisa can tell it's making him horny.

"Where is everybody?" Achton asks.

"Who is everybody?" Alisa answers with a sheepish smile. "The night is ours," she says.

"It must have cost you a fortune to rent this place out. How can I ever repay you?"

"Would you repay me, if you had the chance?" Seductively, Alisa sips more of her drink.

"Yes, I will do anything for you Alisa. You've been such a breath of fresh air, not only to me but to Chelsey as well. I really appreciate you and I'm glad you are in our lives." There is a crack in Achton's voice. If he blinks a tear will easily drip from his eye.

"If you really, mean that…"

"I do, Alisa. I really mean it. I know you have met some fucked up people in your life but I'm not like them." Alisa's eyes tear up on cue. It's like the emotions in Achton are so high Alisa can feel them leap from him right into her eyes.

"It's hard to believe you when I'm fighting for my life and you can easily make things easier on me, but you haven't." Alisa takes the napkin from her lap and wipes her eyes.

"Don't cry. It pains me to see you cry." Achton jumps up from his seat ready to comfort Alisa but she stops him with her hand.

"I have a confession to make Alisa," Achton exhales tiredly. "I contemplated on if I should say anything or not." Alisa's ears are more attentive than they look. To Achton, she appears to be sobbing off into her own problems but in reality, she's all ears to his.

"It's like this; I have Chelsey to think about. I don't have money to just throw around. If Monroe is found guilty of any of these charges the benefits me and Chelsey are getting comes to a halt…"

"If it's money you need, I can help you with that. I promise you I'm not trying to take from your child's mouth. I just have to think about my freedom here. I didn't do anything to deserve this. I'm innocent, don't you believe me?" Alisa cries out as the waitress brings over their custom ordered food: steak, broccoli, loaded bake potatoes and hot fresh rolls.

"Yes, I believe you Alisa. That's my confession. Initially, I couldn't see Monroe doing the things you were accusing her of but as time grew, I started to find out things about my wife that I had no idea about. It's like I was married to a fuckin stranger all these years," Achton takes a deep breath before he says his next sentence.

"I found some letters…I found a suicide letter from Monroe and in the letter, she basically tells me how she was going to make things right for our family no matter what."

"What else did she say?" Alisa asks.

"Just know, I believe you Alisa. My word is my bond and I'm telling you, I got you. I won't let you down." This time Alisa jumps up from the table and twists right over to Achton.

"Are you saying that I can trust you?" Alisa straddles Achton's lap and whispers into his ear.

"I keep saying the same thing over and over, woman," Achton jokes but he never gives Alisa his word. Smoothly, Alisa unzips Achton's slacks and pulls his penis out.

"Do you know what I'm in the mood for?" she seductively whispers into his ear.

"Right here, right now in front of the entire staff?" Alisa slides her dress up and without warning slips Achton's dick into her hole and like a cowgirl she rode him to victory. Right there in front of the staff, Achton and Alisa make love like they are the only two in the room.

CHAPTER 24

Quietly, Patricia takes Jason's dick from his boxer-shorts. He's deep into his sleep but she knew just the thing to wake him up. She begins to palm his penis in her hand. His dick is throbbing, and veins are popping out of it everywhere. He looks so yummy to Patricia, she moans, "Umm, baby," she takes the base of his dick in her hand and begins to squeeze it gently. Eyes still glued shut; he takes her head and begins pumping his dick into her mouth fast and furiously.

As Patricia takes his balls into her mouth and bounces them on her tongue, Jason moans out, "I'm about to cum, baby. Aww!"

Patricia can hardly wait. His warm nectar shoots out, and Patricia slurps it up with her tongue.

"Hmmm, you taste so good, baby," Patricia jumps up from the bed and runs to the bathroom to clean out her mouth. She returns with a warm rag to wipe away the left-over nut from Jason's penis.

"See, being back home isn't so bad," he jokes, and Patricia bursts into laughter.

"I guess I'm alright. I just hate the thought of someone being in my house, all in my personal things, destroying my home when I'm not here. It's no telling what the hell they did while we were gone," Patricia lays her head flat onto Jason's chest. Her ear is pressed to his heartbeat.

"I love you; Patricia and I appreciate your patience with me. I promise I will not fuck up this time." Patricia lifts her head and turns to look Jason in his eyes. She really feels his serenity and she wants him to know she trusts him.

"I forgive you, Jason. I just want us to start fresh. I don't want to go into our marriage with old baggage. I forgive you and I hope you forgive me."

Jason jumps in and says, "Baby, you haven't done anything. It's been me with the stupid stuff."

Patricia tries to shake her guilt, *Oh, I'm not the angel you think I am*, she reflects. The night with Mr. Sexy invades her thoughts. She can barely stand the thought of it. *What was I thinking?*

"I just know, there is a reason you've been acting out. Only I don't know what the reason is. If I'm not doing something or doing something wrong, I'd rather you tell me so we can talk it over, you know?" Jason takes his hand and rubs his fingers through Patricia's weave.

"Communication is the key to longevity, when it comes to friendships. Best friends, boyfriend and girlfriend and most definitely husband and wife." Patricia lifts her head to look and see if Jason is listening to her.

"Patricia, you haven't done anything baby. I just have to get my shit together and I am. I love you too much to lose you." Jason lifts half-way from the bed to kiss Patricia on her forehead.

"I love you too Jason."

"I know you love me, Patricia. You better!" he jokes before flipping her over on her back. Repeatedly, he kisses her on the forehead, nose, cheek and finally lips.

"Now, why did you wake me up so early?" Jason rests his body between Patricia's legs. Her breasts are the best pillows.

"I couldn't sleep, and I wanted you to wake up with me," Patricia giggles a little then pulls Jason's face in close and begin to kiss him.

When Jason finally gets a chance to breath, he says, "Can I get some breakfast, woman?"

"Where is the maid when you need one?" Patricia jokes, remembering Jason telling her how he wanted her to be his wife and not his cook.

"I'll hire her back, baby. I just didn't want to seem so controlling." *Who is this new Jason, and can I keep him?* Patricia thinks as she jumps up from the bed.

"I was just joking, baby. I don't mind. I'll whip up something real quick."

"Thank you."

Jason turns down the hallway leading to the kitchen and immediately the beautiful aroma assaults him: eggs, bacon, cheese grits and butter biscuits.

"You're finally dressed, male diva?" Patricia says to Jason as he takes a seat at the bar. Jason pinches his index finger and thumb together. "Ah, now this is what I'm talking about!" he shouts happily, rubbing his six-pack.

"You so crazy," Patricia says before sliding his plate closer to him.

"Baby, are we still going to your folks' cabin this weekend?"

"Yes, we are still going. And it's our cabin now. My parents gifted it to us as a wedding present. They just bought themselves a new one."

Patricia claps her hands like a kid and shouts out, "Yay! I always wanted a cabin!"

"Well, now you have one," Jason adds.

"I'm so excited and I'm glad we're not going through with the big wedding deal. The more I think about it, you were right. It would just be so inconvenient right now. Plus, in five years, we'll be able to have our daughter...."

"Or son," Jason chimes in to say.

"Or son, in our wedding, we'll be settled and in a place where we can just focus on the wedding and not all the other complications newlyweds deal with."

"I'm glad you agree baby."

"Well, I have to go Jason. I'm not going to be in the office long today. So, I need to get an early start."

"You're not pulling an all-nighter today? Whaaaat!" Jason jokes.

"No. I don't feel too good. Actually, I feel horrible. I'm just going to get some paperwork and then I'm bringing my work back home."

"What's wrong?" Jason asks before sticking a spoon full of grits in his mouth.

"Nothing. Just some girl stuff," Patricia says.

"Okay, well take my truck today. I need to go get the oil changed on car while I got some free time."

"Okay." Patricia prances over to Jason, plants a big kiss on his lips, and skips out the house.

"I love you!" he yells out.

"I love you too, Jason," she blurts from the other side of the door.

CHAPTER 25

Quickly, the young lady swallows the Ativan and waits for it to kick in. Once she sets foot out the car it will be too late to turn around. Her anxiety is getting the best of her. Already her heart rate is accelerating, and her mind is replaying the many things that can go wrong. With her conscious mind, she silently repeats a chant to herself: *I will not hurt anyone. I'm not leaving here with blood on my hands. I am a child of God. God please forgive me.*

Twenty minutes later, she and her partner are pulling up to their destination. Her stomach heaves unhelpfully but the meds help keep a lid on her nerves.

"Listen, we are in and out. Don't say my mutha-fuckin' name and don't take off your fucking mask!" Swiftly, he jumps out the car and leads the way. Hesitantly, she follows. Every footstep near the house feels like a step towards her own grave. Already her heart is pounding and her forehead beneath the mask is sweating. Her chanting: *I will not hurt anyone. I'm not living here with blood on my hands. I am a child of God. God please forgive me* is louder than her negative thoughts.

Jason suddenly wakes up. Is that a noise in the house, or part of his dream? In his dream, Jason is about to kiss Patricia. He looks around the house, but he sees nothing. Determined to get a nap in, he lays back down in the bed to resume his nap. Slowly, Jason feels his body start to relax and his mind drifts back to sleep. He hopes he can return to the dream he'd been having about Patricia, his beautiful, loving fiancée. More and more he's starting to appreciate her. The way she works so hard to prove her worth in their work field, how she puts everyone's needs before her own. The strut in her walk, the confidence in her appearance. In the beginning of their relationship, he'd been crazy about Patricia. He doesn't know why he broke her heart but he's ready to spend the rest of his life putting the pieces back together. Like never before, he can't get her off his mind.

Out of nowhere, there she is, smack in the middle of his dream. He'd been just about to finally kiss her when the loud noise had startled him awake. Falling asleep again, Jason cannot recover the soft kiss he hoped for. Instead, he finds himself stuck in the middle of a dream about bats. In his dream, Jason stands in a dark-black alley; the smell of urine is horrid. He's struggling to fight off the vicious bats, running up and down the alley, screaming, "*Get off me!*"

"*Don't run from them!*"

Jason struggles to see the young lady's face. As she takes a few steps closer, he finally recognized her as the girl who had helped him break Patricia's heart. The girl who played a hand in ruining his relationship. It's Robin. She's standing like a dream in the flesh. Her body is wrapped in a trench coat. Jason is almost certain there is nothing beneath it. Her jet-black bob is chin length and there is a tattoo of a heart on the back of her left hand.

"*There isn't much you can do to stop bats,*" Robin says to Jason before pulling him out from the circle of bats.

"*Do you miss me, Jason?*" Before Robin can kiss Jason, he hears the noise again. This time he opens his eyes and sits up in bed. He looks at the clock on his bedside table. It's twelve o'clock noon. The noise must be Patricia coming back home from work.

Jason is about to lie back down when he remembers that Patricia had only been gone for about twenty-minutes. She wouldn't come back home that fast. Patricia can't be the noise he hears moving around downstairs. Is there someone else in the house, or are his mind playing tricks on him? Quietly, he steps off the bed and tiptoes to the bedroom door.

"Patricia, is that you?" Jason yells as he puts his hand on the doorknob. He slowly pushes the door open and steps out the room with caution.

"Patricia!" he yells again. Jason stops in his tracks when he sees a black masked man standing in the hall with a gun pointed at him. Before he can turn to run back into the room, a single shot rings out hitting him in the knee, causing him to crumble. The tall intruder with a model's physique steps over him with two black .45's in his hand.

"Please don't kill me! Please! If its money you want, you can have it. Look in the safe in the closet!" Jason pleads out holding his knee.

"Your money is not good here." Before Jason catches the next bullet in his stomach, he notices the beautiful red heart on the back of the second masked person's left hand.

"Aww," he moans out holding his stomach tightly. Third shot....

"Aww!" the young lady screams out. Forth shot... "No, stop it!" she blurts out. Five... Jason is out cold.

"Stop all that damn screaming and come help me get his body to the car." Fearful, she helps him with the body, grabbing his arms while he grabbed Jason's legs. Out the house and through the garage they drag his body and tuck it in the trunk. Quickly, they clean the blood from the house leaving a large amount blood behind.

Fear is like a knife twisting at the young lady's gut. She's sweating bullets. They can't get to the cabin fast enough. Fear has her in shackles; she can barely focus. Fear is a constant hammer on her head and she's beginning to get a headache.

"I think you need to slow down before we get pulled over by the police," she utters out with a stutter.

"I got this, just chill," he says. After thirty long minutes, they finally arrive at the secluded cabin.

"Are you sure this is it?" he asks her.

"Yes, I think," she answers.

"You think? Shit!" he blurts before jumping out the car. Checking his surroundings, he sees no one. His eyes gaze right over the old lady three cabins down peeking out her window. He pops the trunk and snatches the body out.

"Get your ass out and help me!"

"Will you keep your damn voice down?" she whispers, grabbing a leg and an arm. Together they drag Jason's body to the lake and dump it.

"Come on, let's get out here." Quickly, they speed off into the night.

CHAPTER 26

"**S**peed up, go!" You're driving like someone's grandma!" Patricia is stuck on the highway in California traffic and her stomach is boiling. Any wrong move and she's liable to shit her pants. She's been feeling nausea since she left for work thirty-eight minutes ago, and she can barely hold her breakfast down. It's bound to come up and out her mouth or down and her out her ass. Patricia got halfway to work before deciding she wasn't feeling up to it and turned around.

Beyoncé *Dangerously in Love* CD, pauses as Patricia dials out Jason on the loudspeaker. He doesn't answer for the third time.

"What the hell are you doing, man?" she blurts out weaving in and out of traffic.

"Shit, I should have never drunk that damn coffee!" Patricia's stomach sounds like an angry monster. She can feel her bowels moving.

"Please don't; please just stay in a little while longer." She leans to turn down one of her favorite songs, *Signs*. The music and everything else, from the wind outside to the slow traffic, is starting to irritate her soul. She fights the traffic for twelve more minutes and finally she's pulling into Jason's parking lot. As soon as she put the car in park, she snatches up her purse and runs into the house.

"Jason?" she calls out. The garage door is left ajar, casting a white beam into the house.

"Why is that light on and why is this door open?" Patricia mumbles.

"Jason, where are you?" she yells out. It's odd for the garage door to be left open. Patricia and Jason usually keep that door closed throughout the day. Patricia approaches the door and calls out Jason's name again. There is no answer. She pushes the door and it swings open with ease. A blast of air cold streams past her and so does an indescribable smell.

"What is that smell?" she murmurs.

"I can't leave this man alone for ten minutes without him messing up the place." There are a few house items, like the remote control, a picture frame, and her soy wax candles, cast onto the floor in a haphazard fashion. Patricia thinks, *I wish this man would pick up things when he see them falls.* Patricia is about to close the door and rush to the restroom when she spies Jason's cell phone on the floor with spatters of red blood around it. She picks up the phone and sure enough it's Jason's. Hadn't she not been so sick, her normal paranoid ways would've kicked in but she couldn't function straight, her stomach was hurting and all she could think of was emptying the painful waste from her stomach.

"This is why he hasn't been answering the phone. He must have been trying to work on that damn car." she quickly assumed without thought. "I told his ass to let the mechanic handle the work on that car, now he's cut himself up." Patricia murmurs on her rush to the restroom.

"He probably doesn't even know he doesn't have his phone." While releasing her bowels in the toilet, Patricia makes a call to the firm to speak to Jason, but they inform her he hasn't made it in yet. She assumes he's still out trying to get the oil changed.

Her stomach in so much pain, Patricia takes a Pepto Bismol pill and stretches across the bed. Waiting for the pill to kick in, she easily drifts into dreamland.

"Fuck!" Patricia shouts when she opens her eyes and looks around her bedroom. She notices the clock reads ten o'clock. A wave of nausea shoots in the pit of her gut and she can't move. Her heart is racing, as if she's been running. Her forehead is wet and so are her pajamas. The horrid nightmare of Jason dying in a car wreck has her shook. Her feet are tingling, they've falling asleep. They are dangling over the bed; she shakes them awake.

Patricia stretches across the bed and then wipes her eyes clean. Her phone is close by, she looks at it and notices there are no calls from Jason. She checks his phone and there are no missed calls on his phone either. She jumps up from the bed when she feels vomit rushing up, but nothing comes up when she reaches the bathroom. She figures she needs to put something in her stomach, so she rushes to the kitchen to fix her something to eat.

Two hours later, there is still no sign of Jason and Patricia is starting to get worried. No one from work has seen him today; he hasn't called to check in. It's going on twelve o'clock and he's never been out this late. She picks up the phone, because the police are the only people left she can think to call. His parents haven't heard from him and neither have his siblings. Just as she is dialing the 911, there is a knock on the door.

"I'm going to kill his ass!" she blurts as she ends the call and speed walks to the door.

"Where the hell have you been?" she yells as she slings the door open.

"Hey, ma'am, how are you?" the two officers ask. Both officers tip their hats and nod hello to her. Patricia wonders what they were doing at her house. Whatever it is, she knows it isn't good.

"Ma'am can we come in?" Patricia's heartbeat increases. The anticipation is killing her. She moves to the side to let the officers in.

"How can I help you officers?" Patricia follows them through the foyer.

"Ma'am would you like to take a seat?" one of the officers asks.

"No. In fact, you guys can stop in your tracks and tell me what you want, now!" Patricia says. The officers take a deep breath and one just comes right out and says it.

"The only information we have is that your fiancé has been shot and his body was dumped at his cabin."

Patricia's ears go deaf. She's weak at the knees. The younger officer wants to reach out to hug Patricia tight, but he knows that behavior isn't in the code book and it probably wouldn't help anyway.

"I'm sorry for your loss. We'll have more information for you soon. In the meantime—"

"Just leave!" Patricia blurts out. "I'm sorry. I don't mean to yell." The officers nod their heads.

"It's okay ma'am, we understand." The officers take one sympathetic look at Patricia and then they show themselves out the door. Patricia follows behind the officers and locks the door. She pushes her shoulder blades against the grooves on the door. She's going down in an elevator and it won't stop. But then it does. The door to her heart opens and then here comes the heartache. She feels the thud. Slowly, her acid tears drip from her eyes down her cheeks, resting on her neck. There is a tear in her chest. Her elbows are getting heavy.

She can't stop herself from keeling over, so she goes ahead and rolls into a knot, but find herself unable to stop rocking. She wants to sit back up, but she just can't. Even when she suddenly feels like she's freezing, she can't get up. All she can do is look around the room and hear how loud the silence is already. Her life is over. She's alone, again. This is not the way she dreamed her life would be. This is not the happily-ever-after she prayed for. She wants to fast forward her life to her happy place, but God has the remote.

She can't stomach Jason never walking back into her door anymore. The pain he must've encountered, the thoughts he must've had during his last seconds alive. She would ask who would do such a thing, but she knew the answer, Alisa. She never asked for this torture, all she's ever done is her job. Jason didn't deserve this either. Patricia finally burst into crying when she realizes Jason will never wrap his arms around her again. She'll never smell his heavenly scent or feel his touch. Tonight, and every night from here on out will be a lonely night.

"God, help me please!" she cries out.

CHAPTER 27

Patricia's body sways with the movement of the desk chair, a lazy and understated rocking motion. Her eyes are walking from Alisa hair line to her feet and back up again. Livid, she is staring at the computer screen with so much anger. The only time her gaze breaks is when she has to blink her eyes. Alisa has successfully taken everything she's ever loved away from her and she must pay. The white in Patricia's eyes turns a pure black. If Alisa was there in the flesh, Patricia's lethal stare would painfully pierce through her soul.

After calling Jason's family, *The Hawk*, and Jamellah, to inform them of Jason's death, Patricia locks down. She stops answering phone calls and she takes her spare key from under the mat outside, so no one would invite themselves in. She wants to be alone. Her only focus is to remain focused on the case. Alisa serving time is the only way she figures she'll be able to rest. The only way she can peacefully grieve Jason's death, is if Alisa is put away.

Chelsey places her trembling hand on the Bible. "You do solemnly state that the testimony you may give in the case now pending before this court shall be the truth, the whole truth, and nothing but the truth, so help you God?" The court deputy asks.

Will my mother hate me for what I'm about to do? Would she prefer I lie, or would she be proud of me for telling the truth? God will surely understand. Chelsey raises her eyes to look at her father. He grins, nods his head and lip syncs, *you got this.* Chelsey's testament can set Alisa free, but what choice does she have? She's under oath. Her voice is light and timid.

"I do," she drops her eyes to the dusty floorboards of the courtroom.

"Chelsey, who is Monroe Gosling to you?"

"She's my mother," Chelsey stutters.

"And what would you rate your mother on a scale one to ten, ten being the best?" Chelsey's eyes survey the room. It feels like a million eyes are staring at her, all curious about her thoughts. A presentation of good and bad memories flash through her mind. Her mother wasn't perfect, she concludes, but she knows from experience she had a good heart.

"I would give her an eight," Chelsey answers.

"Why an eight? Why not a ten?" Patricia asks.

"Because, I don't believe any one is perfect. Plus, she could have been home more. Sometimes I felt like she liked working more than being a mother." Chelsey drops her head; she's embarrassed of her comments.

"It's okay, Chelsey. No one here is judging you. You're not on trial. I'm sure your mother wouldn't have wanted you to do anything less than tell the truth today." Patricia hands Chelsey a Kleenex. She knows there will be tears after her next question.

"I'm going to ask you something, but I want you to know, it's not to torture you." The court is quiet, and everyone is watching very attentively. The only sound is Patricia's heels clicking back and forth.

"Do you think your mother killed Dawson, her secret lover?"

"Objection, Your Honor! That is a matter of an opinion. Factually, how would she know?" Kelly pops up from her seat and says.

"You Honor, she lived with this woman, her mother, all of her life. If anyone knows what Detective Gosling is capable of, it's her family. Chelsey has stated early before that her mother isn't perfect, she's even stated why she believes she isn't, and we believed her. So, why can't we ask her if her mother is capable of murder? She's fully aware that she's under oath and knows how important the truth is today," Patricia snaps back, pushing her luck. Secretly praying the Judge will back her up.

"I'll allow it. Answer the question young lady."

Alisa's head lawyer, Grier taps Kelly on the shoulder and then lip syncs, *it's okay, sit down.*

"Thank you, Your Honor," Patricia says before exhaling. She knows without doubt children have the biggest impact on the jury and Chelsey's crying eyes can help her case big time. *I mean who wouldn't cry at the sound of their parent being accused of murder*, Patricia thinks before Chelsey replies.

"I don't know!" Chelsey blurts out before a dam of tears burst from her navy-blue eyes. The court is in chaos. Everyone is chattering and Kelly relaxes suddenly. Patricia looks deep into Chelsey's eyes, but she can't see anything. The child is hard to read. She doesn't know why she's crying. Is it because her mother is capable of murder, or because her mother is being accused of murder?

"Order!" The Judge yells out, banging his gavel.

"Can you elaborate a little more for the jury, Chelsey? What don't you know?" Patricia's heartbeat suddenly increases. She secretly hopes her confused but hopeful stare will bring Chelsey over to the bright side, but if Chelsey secretly hates her mother for cheating on her father, it'll never work.

"I don't know what my mother is capable of. The woman I knew was a lie. The woman I called my mother would have never cheated on my father. She would have never killed herself. So, no, I don't know if my mother killed her secret lover. As much as I'd like to say she wouldn't, it wouldn't be my honest opinion." Like a ticking bomb ready to explode, Chelsey finally breaks into the loudest cry.

Patricia isn't just looking at Chelsey but through her, it's like her head is transparent and she is fascinated by an object two inches behind her skull. Her eyes, that were once hopeful, fell into helplessness. The thought of losing this case turns Patricia stomach every bit as badly as losing Jason.

Chelsey can tell from Patricia's long glare, she's angry with her. Her cold stare screams, *I hate you little girl and I'll never forgive you for this.*

"I'm done with the witness Your Honor," Patricia murmurs before walking back to her seat like a sick mummy.

"The court will take a recess and we will resume after lunch." The Judge bangs his gavel and set the court free.

After reassuring his daughter, she did the right thing, Achton is confident with his decision to do the same thing. He raises his right hand, eager to get the testimony over with.

"You do solemnly state that the testimony you may give in the case now pending before this court shall be the truth, the whole truth, and nothing but the truth, so help you God?" the court deputy asks.

"I do."

Patricia decides to take a different route after Chelsey's testimony. She can't afford to come at Achton from the same angle.

"Mr. Gosling, did you love your wife Monroe Gosling?"

"Yes, of course I did." Immediately, Achton can feel Patricia's bad vibe. He can tell she isn't going to be as easy on him as she was on Chelsey but he's fine with that. Better him than Chelsey, he figures.

"How did you feel when you found out about detective Gosling's affair?"

"I was furious and very heart-broken." Attentive and very focused, Kelly listens closely to Patricia's questions.

"Would you ever expect your wife to cheat on you?"

"No, I was completely blind-sided. I thought for sure we were happy."

"Did you hate her for her betrayal?" Patricia paces back and forth, twirling a pen around her fingers.

"I mean who wouldn't hate their spouse for cheating?"

Patricia stops in front of the witness stand and blurts, "Yes or no, Mr. Gosling. Did you hate your wife for cheating on you?"

"Yes, I hated her for it, okay!" Patricia nods her head.

"Okay, I hear you loud and clear. Do you hate your wife enough to say she killed her secret lover, even if you're not sure she did?" Achton doesn't like the new Patricia, at all. He badly wants to curse her out like he would anybody who tried him with the wrong tone, but he knew that would end up with him somewhere he didn't want to be; jail.

"No! I would never put something like that on her. I hated her for what she did to our family, but I also forgave her before her dying day!" Achton blurts out.

"So, you don't believe she killed her secret lover, Dawson?"

"Yes, I believe she did it. I'm sure of it." Patricia is stunned as well as the rest of the courtroom. No one was prepared for Achton's answer, but Kelly is loving every bit of it.

"How can you be so sure, Mr. Gosling? Is this your way of getting payback on your wife, damaging her reputation that she cared so much about?"

"No! I would never do that."

"Then, how can you be so sure, Mr. Gosling?" Patricia snaps.

"Because she left a letter," he blurts. The courtroom once again turns into chaos.

"Order! Order! I will have order in this court, now!"

"You Honor, I'd like to approach the bench," Patricia says.

"Approach, Ms. Patterson." Both Kelly and Patricia approach the bench.

"I don't know what's going here, but my witness never said anything about a letter to me. I need to read this letter, and have it examined for fingerprints." The judge looks over to Kelly, who has no objections.

"Okay, I'll allow you the time."

"Thank you, Your Honor," Patricia says before strutting away.

"I will allow the court time to look over this letter and to examine it for fingerprints. Until then, court will recess. You may step down." The judge turns to say to Achton.

"And young man, you are ordered to give that letter to Ms. Patterson."

"Yes sir," Achton replies. Alisa smiles sheepishly at Patricia on her way on the courtroom. Patricia knows something is up, but again, she doesn't know what exactly. Alisa has done it again. She's out slicked the slicker.

CHAPTER 28

S lowly, Patricia pulls into her driveway. Almost instantly, she wants to turn around. On her porch awaiting her arrival are Jamellah and Nichole.

"Why can't they get the picture already?" she mumbles before putting the car in park. Jamellah is holding what seems to be a bag of Chinese food and Nichole is holding a bag from JJ's liquor store. It's clear these two have no intention of going home.

"What are you cows doing here?" Patricia yells out as soon as she shuts the car door behind her.

"We are here to give you moral support, that's what." Jamellah stands on her feet as Patricia nears.

"That's sweet y'all, it really is, but I told y'all, I'm dealing with this my way."

"Patricia, your way is being alone and that's not safe nor healthy. I read somewhere…" Both Patricia and Jamellah turn to face Nichole.

Patricia drops her head, toots her lips, and raises her eyebrows, "Really Nichole? You're going to give me tips on how to grieve my fiancé's death from a book you read?" Jamellah burst into laughter and like a domino effect, Patricia joins her.

"I'm serious, it really works." Nichole follows the girls into the house.

"Nichole, when have you had to grieve?" Jamellah asks.

"When I was grieving Daphne, tips from this book really helped me."

"A dog, Nichole?" Jamellah jokes.

"Hey, dogs are no different from humans." As much as Patricia hates to admit it, her girlfriends' presence was already taking her mind off her horrible day in court.

"The lady who wrote this book was a grieving widow, and she basically jotted down things that helped her through her tough time," Nichole says.

"And what was one thing she said that you think would help me?" Patricia flops onto her sofa to kick off the heels that have her feet screaming.

"She said often times, you're going to feel like you are alone and don't want to be bothered…"

"Oh, maybe she does know what she's talking about," Patricia chimes in to say.

"But, she says you shouldn't push love or good company away but instead drown in it," Nichole finishes her sentence with a collar flip.

"I don't know, maybe this…what's her name, has a point," Jamellah adds. Patricia toots her lips once again and then rolls her eyes at both her homegirls.

"Y'all, really, I'm good. I just need to finish this case and when it's over, I'm going to grieve my man peacefully."

"Through all this, all you can think about is this case, Patricia?" Nichole snaps.

"You just lost the love of your life. Don't they give you like vacation leave or something?" Nichole continues.

"Yes, I can hand the case over if I want to, but I don't. It'll be like suicide and I refuse to let this bitch off that easy…" Before Jamellah can add her statement, Patricia stops her with her hand.

"No, let me finish! I will not be able to put Jason to rest until this bitch is put away. Do y'all not understand that she is behind his death? All my pain falls back on her. Shit, putting her away, is me grieving!"

"I understand your point, but we're not leaving." Jamellah reaches into the bag and pulls out a box of shrimp fried rice.

"Do you want the shrimp, chicken or house friend rice?" she asks Patricia.

"I'll take the house fried rice," she replies.

"Cool, Nichole you can get the chicken." Nichole refuses the box.

"How come, you pick what I want?" Nichole says.

"Because I want the shrimp, so chicken is what's left." The girls burst into laughter. Nichole stares at the box for ten long seconds and then finally grabs it.

"Well, I'm getting the sweet and sour chicken," Nichole whines.

"Alright, cry baby," Jamellah says.

"Patricia, you can get the spicy bourbon." Jamellah hands Patricia her plate of food.

"Dang, that was quick. Things got back to normal fast. What happen to me getting first pick?" Patricia jokes.

"Oh, I'm sorry baby, do you want the BBQ?" Jamellah asks with her baby accent.

"Nope, it's too late now. I don't even want first pick anymore," Patricia joins the act and responds like a spoiled brat. Hours pass as Jamellah, Patricia and Nichole share laughs and heart-to-heart conversations. Then there are the moments when the room gets silent and extremely awkward. Both the girls wished Patricia would just cry already, but she doesn't. Instead, she flips through her Black Berry doing God knows what.

"So, who's going to do the funeral arrangements?" Nichole breaks the silence and asks.

"Well his mother is handling everything, so I'll just do my part and show up." Jamellah can tell Patricia is bothered.

"Would you have rather do the arrangements?" Jamellah asks.

"Well, that was our agreement. If I went first he would have done mine."

"Over my dead body," Jamellah murmurs.

"What you say?" Patricia asks Jamellah.

"Oh, nothing girl but, it's probably a good thing you don't have to be bothered with all that, you know? Especially, since you're on trial and everything," Patricia and Nichole nod their heads.

"Yeah, I guess you're right," Patricia says right before her phone rings.

"Hold on for a second, I got to take this," she jumps up from the couch and wanders off into the hall.

"The fingerprints came back positive," David says.

"What?" Patricia yells.

"Monroe wrote the letter," David mumbles. He knows this is not the news Patricia is hoping for and he hates he's the one to break the bad news to her.

"Wow!" she says before ending the call. Like a track star, Patricia shoots up the stairs and slams the bedroom door behind her. The girls watch each other silently for about twenty seconds before they hear the most hysterical crying. The screaming sobs are only interrupted by Patricia's need to draw breath. It's a primal sound, one any decent human being is programmed not to ignore.

Jamellah and Nichole turn their heads towards the staircase, caught between an impulse to help and another to stay clear. Should they allow their friend time to mourn, cry, and feel bad for herself? Whatever they decide, their day has been altered. To be so close to such pain changes a person, even if just temporarily. Their own pains comes a little closer to the surface; their empathy is triggered. If they choose to walk away, they get a little kick of guilt as a punishment, a sharp jab to guide them to do the right thing next time around. If they choose to say they get a little kick of guilt as well, thus they may be blamed for being overbearing, selfish and inconsiderate.

"What should we do?" Nichole turns to ask Jamellah. She shrugs her shoulders in confusion first and then after a minute answers, "Let's just let her cry for a minute and we'll check on her after she has cried some." Nichole nods her head in agreement and then turns her attention back to the staircase. Like a kid being dropped off at daycare, Patricia cries her heart out.

CHAPTER 29

"This court, ladies and gentlemen, council. I want to thank you all for the time you've spent with this case. I know that it has been a very trying trial," Patricia turns to the jury as she recites her closing argument.

"The opposite of oppressor, is pray. A victim is what the defendant wants you to believe she is. She wants you to believe a law-abiding citizen and officer of the courts threatened her to kill her husband. The husband she caught cheating on her, the husband who used her for money, the husband who wanted out of a suffering marriage.

"The defendant wants you to believe that she didn't kill her husband out of revenge, but because his mistress told her to. There is a difference between what constitutes reasonable doubt, and what amounts to just excuses by the defendant. Ladies and gentlemen of the jury, the defendant sought revenge that night for her broken heart. The law doesn't allow a woman to get revenge and then create motives for others who may have wanted the same revenge." Attentively, the jury is listening. Their eyes are following Patricia's every move.

"We've heard witnesses say that they've witnessed Mr. Hopkins alive and healthy before entering a house, our defendant's house," Patricia points over to Alisa.

"That same witness, witnessed Mr. Hopkins being toted out that same house on the same day, in a body bag. That same witness heard with their own ears the shooting." Patricia pulls the pen from her ear and slams it into her palm after every fact.

"Let's see, her house, her gun, her bullets, and plenty of motives. This case is not about what we believe, but what we see. And what we see is evidence that is clearly stating that Dawson's murderer is right here in this courtroom.

"There is a saying that actions speak louder than words. We ask you to judge the defendant by her actions, by what she did that night, not by what she said today in the courtroom. Her claims today do not match her actions on the day in question. We are a nation of laws, and every citizen is obliged to follow those laws. Today, let's bring justice to the forefront for Mr. Dawson Hopkins and put away his wife, Alisa Hopkins, for she believed that law didn't apply to her the night she killed her husband. Thank you."

Patricia flops into her seat, confident in her closing. If she loses, it'll be because the jury was blind and not because she didn't give it her best. The court is set for recess and Patricia leaves for lunch a drink. The Hennessey and coke helps take the stress away. Three hours later, she is back in court waiting for a verdict. Silently, she sits in her crisp suit, her folded half-moon glasses bouncing up and down on her knee as she taps her foot. Her four-inch heels bang on the striking wooden courtroom floor. On every third bounce or so, she catches herself but within seconds, she starts back. Earlier before trial, Patricia's black hair fell loose and wavy to the small of her back, but now it's tied tightly into a bun. The only movements on her head are the large gold hoop earrings. She imagines herself to appearing calm and collected, but her leg gives her away.

"Jury, how do you find the defendant on the charge of first degree murder?"

The white thin brunet pulls her glasses down to read from the paper. "We the jury find the defendant Alisa Hopkins, not guilty,"

Patricia is in disbelief; she can barely swallow. *I failed him*; she thinks before flopping back into the desk chair. The court is in an uproar. Some people are cheering, and some are just plain out angry. Alisa's eyes are trained on some invisible ghost, her heavy eyelids a fraction too slow to blink, her irises too stationary. It's as if her brain is suffering a massive short circuit and is struggling to compute.

Kelly moves into her line of sight, tapping her on the shoulder with her left hand, her lips forming a pensive grin. Alisa's head tilts upward to her face, her eyes sliding into focus.

"We did it, you're a free woman." Alisa breaks from her robotic aura and hugs Kelly tightly.

"Patricia, we got trouble outside," David whispers into Patricia's ear on the way out the courtroom.

"What do you mean?" she asks.

"Listen, just whatever you do; don't say anything, okay?"

"What are talking about, David?" Before David can answer Patricia, she's greeted by LAPD outside the courtroom.

"Patricia Patterson, you are under arrest for the murder of Jason Beachum."

"What?" Patricia blurts out as the officer place her in handcuffs.

"You have got to be kidding me, right now?"

"Patricia, just keep quiet," David blurts out.

"What the hell is going on?" No one has an answer for Patricia. Instead the officer continues reading her rights.

"You have the right to remain silent. Anything you say can and will be used against you in a court of law. You have the right to an attorney. If you cannot afford an attorney, one will be provided for you. Do you understand the rights I have just read to you?"

"Ooch!"

"Yo, be careful with how you handle her!" David yells out at the officer. On-lookers and the news reporters are following behind the officers and Patricia closely. Snapping pictures and asking dumb questions. On the way out the door, Patricia locks eyes with Alisa. She gives her a sheepishly grin and nods her head.

"You bitch!" Patricia blurts out.

"I hate you!" Patricia screams as the officers tuck her away into the police car. Blankly, Alisa stares at Patricia ranting hateful words to her from the police car before she is hauled away.

NEXT ON "THE DEFENSE"

NATIONAL BESTSELLING AUTHOR

CORNELIA SMITH

www.ingramcontent.com/pod-product-compliance
Lightning Source LLC
Chambersburg PA
CBHW071959170626
46813CB00005B/1932